processing
the computer
conspiracy

processing the computer conspiracy

SUMMIT HIGH SERIES

Matt Tullos

BROADMAN & HOLMAN PUBLISHERS

Nashville, Tennessee

0-8054-0181-4

Published by Broadman & Holman Publishers, Nashville, Tennessee
Page Design: Anderson Thomas, Nashville, Tennessee
Typesetter: PerfecType, Nashville, Tennessee
Acquisitions & Development Editor: Janis Whipple

Dewey Decimal Classification: F
Subject Heading: HIGH SCHOOLS—FICTION
Library of Congress Card Catalog Number: 97-40331

Scripture used is taken from TLB, The Living Bible, copyright © Tyndale House Publishers, Wheaton, Ill., 1971, used by permission.

Library of Congress Cataloging-in-Publication Data
Tullos, Matt, 1963–
    Processing the computer conspiracy / Matt Tullos.
        p.   cm. — (Summit High series ; 2)
    Summary: When a group of friends happen to see suspicious activity outside
their high school late one night, they get caught up in the incident in ways
requiring courage and faith.
    ISBN 0-8054-0181-4 (tp)
    [1. Christian life—Fiction. 2. Courage—Fiction. 3. High schools—Fiction.
4. Schools—Fiction.] I. Title. II. Series: Tullos, Matt, 1963–   Summit High series ; 2.
PZ7.T82316Pr 1998
[Fic]—dc21

                                                                97-40331
                                                                     CIP
                                                                      AC

1 2 3 4 5 02 01 00 99 98

Dedication

To Mark and Lillie Rose

Closing time finally arrived Friday night at the BurgeRama, "A Retro Burger Boutique." The slightly overpriced hamburger haven sat next to the Regal 12 Cinema and found its most hectic periods shortly after the early evening shows. The music blaring through the speakers was an eclectic mix of Chuck Berry, Elvis Costello, the B-52s, and Bill Halley and the Comets. Clipper, Justin, Autumn, and Kandi were finishing the late shift.

"If I hear 'Rock Around the Clock' one more time," Clipper said, flipping the burgers over the flaming grill, "I think I'm gonna puke."

"Please, Clipper, not on the grill," Justin said.

"You guys are sick," Autumn laughed.

The four friends always asked to work together, and they did well as a team. Their weekend work was partly for the money, but mostly for fun.

Clipper and Justin had been friends for years. Autumn and Kandi were close though they had known each other only for a couple of months.

Justin had partied and generally caused trouble his first two years at Summit High, while keeping up a popular profile among the students. But he walked away from the drinking scene and never returned. He still loved having a good time, but he had a new sense of purpose and passion. His newfound faith cost him some social status. For the first time since coming to Summit, his name wasn't on the nominee list for class favorite.

With long, curly red hair that grew longer as the school year progressed, Clipper, a tall, lean junior, loved life more than most. He tackled it head on, made lots of mistakes, but had very few regrets. Obedient and faithful? Yes, but more than a little off-the-wall. He usually found the perfectly wrong word for most public occasions.

Autumn, the freshman of the group, had dark skin, shoulder-length brown hair, and a delicately soft smile. She was docile, loving, and congenial to all, except when someone mentioned evolution, land mines, or school prayer bans. She was a creationist, pacifist, evangelical freshman.

Kandi, an attractive girl with chestnut hair and an irresistible smile, had moved to Indianapolis a few months earlier when her mom accepted a corporate transfer from Amarillo, Texas. Kandi found her place in Summit High quickly and enjoyed the support of a few close friends. She had recently experienced some difficult times with the divorce of her parents and the sudden move. But now she felt her life had turned around. As a new believer, she was learning daily what her commitment to Christ meant.

Kandi and Autumn were inseparable. They became best friends shortly after Kandi moved to Indianapolis. At first glance, they seemed an unlikely pair, with very few things in common.

Kandi was a fair-skinned Anglo.

Autumn was African-American.

Kandi was a new Christian.

Autumn was a preacher's kid.

Kandi and Justin enjoyed a close friendship and fought the urge to fall head over heels into a starry-eyed dating mode, for fear they would ruin the friendship.

Clipper had an impossible crush on a sophomore named Jenny. He'd only spoken to her a couple of times—small talk while waiting in line for lunch and once while standing around during a fire drill. But Clipper had memorized every millisecond of each encounter. Justin, Kandi, and Autumn had a great time kidding him about his crush. Whenever they were together at school and passed Jenny in the hall, the three would sing Clipper's proper name, "Cliiifoooord."

"Would you guys cut it out!" Clipper would whisper through clenched teeth and his lips tight. "Do you know how irritating that is?"

Clipper stared out the BurgeRama's side window, broom in hand, a strange mixture of hope and dread on his face. He hoped that he would see Jenny come out of the theater and head to the BurgeRama for fries, a shake, or something. Anything that would afford an encounter with her. But strangely, he never saw her except at school.

"Hey, Clipper," Jesse, the weekend manager, said over the conversations of exiting patrons, "the broom can't sweep without your help. It's five minutes till close. Can we get some motion here?"

"Oh, sorry."

"What are you looking at anyway?" Autumn called out from behind the counter.

"Just uh . . . looking. I'm mentally taking a short trip to the Bahamas."

Justin shook his head. "Well, drop the sun block and help me with the fry station when you're through over there."

Clipper finished sweeping the dining area. He passed the handful of remaining customers on his way to the back room. Just before Jesse switched the sign to "Closed," miracle of miracles, Jenny and her parents entered the BurgeRama.

Autumn and Kandi smiled, eyes comically wide.

Jesse said politely, "Sorry, folks, we're—"

Autumn and Kandi screamed in unison, "NO!"

Jesse gave them a strange look. No one ever encouraged latecomers on a Friday night. "Guess what. We're open," he said, forcing a smile then glaring at the duet of opposition. Jenny and her parents slowly walked in looking perplexed.

"Hey, Jenny!" Autumn said.

"Hi!" Jenny said, smiling tentatively, not knowing Autumn's name.

By that time, Kandi shoved Clipper up to the register to take their order.

"What are you doing, Kandi? I told you I don't do change," Clipper said.

"You will this time, Clipper. Believe me you will."

"Why is everybody picking on me tonight?" Clipper whined.

Kandi squeezed his arm and he reacted, "Ouch, you're weird. Didn't I tell you th—HI! May I take your order please?" Clipper's attitude quickly changed.

"Hi, Clipper," Jenny said with a beautiful white smile.

"Oh, hey, Jenny," he stammered, as if he just recognized her. "How's it going? I didn't see you at school today."

"We had to go out of town for a funeral."

"Oh. Um . . . I'm sorry to hear that. Really sorry . . ."

"Just a half uncle of mine."

"Good!" Clipper said, thinking, *Did I say good? I can't believe I said good!* "I mean, I'm glad it wasn't your dad or anything."

"So am I," Jenny's dad interjected dryly.

Justin took their order: Two Bernie Burgers w/ cheese, Charbroiled Chicken Charley, and three Diet Cokes. Kandi, Justin, and Autumn looked on with playful interest. Even Jesse had caught on to the situation and watched intently. Clipper thought, *When did this restaurant turn into the Clipper and Jenny Show?* "Uh, Kandi," he said quietly, "could you come here for a sec?"

"Oh," she broke from her trance, "sure. What's up?"

Clipper turned away from his fantasy customer. He could feel his face turning red as he began his plea for help. "I haven't used that thing in three weeks."

"What thing?"

"The register. I don't want to mess this whole thing up, OK?"

"All right. You get the food, and I'll ring it up. What did they order?"

"Order?"

Kandi rolled her eyes, smiled, and talked slowly as if Clipper were a foreigner. "I think they told you what they wanted to eat. What did they say?"

Clipper looked at her blankly. "I can't remember."

"You're impossible."

Finally when the order and service ritual ended, the trio took the tray to the far corner of the dining area. Jenny looked like she was actually enjoying the confusion. Clipper felt suddenly sad. Jenny's picture perfect smile, and even the way words seemed to roll out of her mouth effortlessly as she quietly talked to her mom, left him stunned silly and engulfed in infatuation. And yet as he looked at the distorted reflection of his face in the stainless steel counter he thought to himself, *The girl's way outta my league.*

Justin pleaded with Clipper, "Go over there and talk to her."

"I can't!"

"Why not?"

"I like her too much," Clipper explained.

"You like her too much so you're not going to talk to her. Hmmm," Kandi interjected sarcastically as she passed the two guys and headed toward the soda fountain.

"I just can't, Justin. She's with her mom and dad."

"That's even better. Get in good with the dad."

"What? Look at me!" Clipper said, noting his white pants with tiny droplets of barbecue sauce and ketchup on his glowing yellow uniform.

"So what?" Justin whispered. "Here's a bright young man, gainfully employed, a little stained and smelly."

"NO WAY!" Clipper decided. The word *smelly* settled the matter for him. He knew he didn't have a chance with Jenny.

The four friends finally clocked out at 11 P.M. They rode together so they could discuss serious stuff as well as off-the-wall analysis of school events and happenings. Usually Justin drove; tonight he let Kandi do the honors because she had just gotten her driver's license.

They all piled into Kandi's mom's '89 Mercury Sable. Someone had jokingly labeled the car by writing Kandi's name on the rear window in pink shoe polish. Kandi started the car and Clipper started talking.

"You're making way too much out of this whole Jenny thing," he said.

"*We're* making too much out of it?" Autumn questioned.

"Way too much. I just think she's cute, and I made the mistake of mentioning it couple of times."

"Make that about five times today," said Justin.

"OK. Fine. I won't ever talk to you about her again!" Clipper vowed.

"Wanna bet?" Kandi proposed.

A brief hush invaded the car as the subject changed. "Clipper," Justin asked, "are you going to need a ride tomorrow night to the rally?"

"You won't have enough room. Dad's letting me take the van for the kidnapping," Clipper replied.

"You're kidding! The new van that you weren't supposed to touch 'til you were forty?" Justin exclaimed.

"Excuse me. I missed something," Autumn said. "What's with the kidnapping?"

"You must not have read the flier our church sent out," Kandi explained. "About an hour before the concert and rally, the youth groups are having a kidnapping contest to see who can grab the most people out of their houses and bring them along."

The last time this happened, Justin was a kidnapping victim. Kidnapped by Clipper and five others, he went to an event that changed the direction of his life. He was still amazed that one crazy event could have such an eternal impact on him.

"Guess who I'm kidnapping tomorrow night?" Clipper asked. "Felix."

"Who's Felix?" Kandi asked.

"You know Felix, don't you? The custodian at Summit?"

"His name's Felix? How'd you know that?" Kandi asked.

"I talk to him all the time."

"OK. Let's get this for the record. Clipper won't talk to Jenny, but he will talk to the janitor," Justin added with a smile.

Clipper defended himself. "He's a really great guy. Kind of slow, but really nice. Believe it or not, I think he's got a lot of wisdom."

The others listened with interest as Clipper recounted the conversations and what he learned about the man. Felix had been the custodian at Summit for over twenty years. He started as a young man and became a faithful employee, proud to be a capable worker, although his mental abilities were less than average. Some of the students made fun of him and called him the local Forrest Gump. But Felix took all comments in stride. He enjoyed being around the students even though most of them never took the time get to know him. Felix worked hard, but he had a tough time keeping track of more than two or three duties at a time. This irritated some of the faculty and administration, who wanted the school to dismiss him for leaving the supply closet open overnight, or failing to clean the shop floor after class projects. In the end, Felix's good heart and intentions always seemed to win the reluctant approval of even the most critical personnel.

Kandi drove down the street that passed by Summit High. Clipper continued, "I can't wait 'til Felix sees me roll up to his house in that van. He's gonna freak."

"Do you think he'll really come?" Autumn asked.

"You bet he will. Why not?"

"All I can say," Kandi said smiling, "is you've really outdone yourself. That's a great idea."

Autumn looked over to the dimly lit parking lot of Summit High and saw headlights flash for about half a second. "Wait. What's that?"

"What's what?" Justin asked.

"Do you see those lights?" Autumn asked.

"What lights?"

"They're off now."

"Guess they are installing new flood lights. Testing them out maybe," Justin suggested.

Autumn cynically replied, "I guess this is as good a time as any."

The dim glow of the school's security lights cast an eerie glow on a splotchy yellow '65 Ford pick-up parked at the side of the main building.

Clipper squinted and replied, "That looks like it might be Lester's truck."

"Yeah, right," Autumn replied.

"Really! I think it is. Can't you tell?"

"Sorry, Clipper. I left my infrared night goggles at home."

"I think you're right, Clipper," Justin added.

"What makes you think that?" Kandi asked.

"Nobody else drives such a monstrosity," Justin replied. Lester's truck suffered from a major paint-matching predicament. Its varied colors included a gross green-yellow and neon banana.

"What's he doing at the school so late?" Autumn asked.

If Justin had been driving, he would have pulled into the front parking lot. "Kandi? Aren't you gonna check it out?"

She shook her head. "Don't be silly. This is my first time out, and I don't want it to be my last. I've got a schedule to keep here."

Clipper threw in a plea. "It's only going to take half a second. I've gotta know what Lester's doing. I smell a rat here. Com'on."

"I promise, just a peek," Justin added.

Kandi got testy. "Why do you guys always figure that Lester's doing something wrong? Can't you let him live his own life? Can't you trust him?"

"About as far as I can throw him," Autumn interjected. Now Kandi felt they were ganging up on her.

"Please, Mom, please," Clipper said in a childlike voice.

Kandi couldn't help but laugh. She gave in and wheeled the car into the last driveway of the high school and coasted slowly through the parking lot.

"All I've got to say is I've got to be home in thirty minutes, or I'll have received and lost my driving privileges in a twelve-hour period."

"A new Indianapolis record," Clipper said in an announcer's voice.

"Wrong. I got my license and lost it in twenty minutes," Justin said.

"Whoa! No way!" Autumn said.

"Yep," Justin replied. "Got a ticket for running a red light on my way home from taking the driving test. I thought the yellow light would last a little longer."

As the car crept forward, Justin gripped the dashboard and peered out the windshield. "I just want a quick look," he said under his breath.

The vehicle came into sight. A moment later, Lester appeared carrying a large box. Seeing his slow and careful movements, Justin decided the box must be heavy. Lester placed it in the bed of the truck, then hurried back to the school entrance. A few seconds later he reappeared with another box. They watched as Lester scrambled back and forth from his truck to the entrance.

Clipper finally broke the silence. "I don't think I've ever seen Lester work that hard. It's a thing of beauty." His voice was filled with awe.

"OK. He's there. He's working hard. Big deal. Let's get out of here before I get the really big deal from Mom." Kandi took her foot off the brake and gently touched the gas.

"No! Wait. Not yet." Justin's voice was urgent. "What's he doing? He's got five of those boxes in his truck. Something smells weird about this whole thing," Justin continued. "I don't think it's a science project."

"What if he's stealing something?" Clipper asked.

"Could we go now?" Kandi whined.

"Yeah," Autumn added her agreement with Kandi.

Clipper proposed that they move up a little closer to the scene. Justin advised against it. "We don't wanna be too nosey."

"You're such a hypocrite. If we aren't nosey, then what are we doing here?" Autumn asked.

"I'd bet you anything something illegal is going on here," Justin said.

Mr. Leafblad, a science teacher, walked out of the side entrance. Neither Lester nor Leafblad noticed the white Sable. Leafblad, a popular teacher among the Summit High student body, gained fame and an off-beat following for his comical lectures on sewage treatment plants. Leafblad was also known for having favored students. Unbelievably, Lester had somehow made that list.

"All bets are off," Justin said as Kandi pressed the gas pedal. "He must be helping Leafblad get ready for summer break or something. Odd couple, if you ask me. Still doesn't look right."

Autumn countered, "You are so suspicious! Mr. Leafblad is probably developing a relationship with Lester so he can have a positive impact on his life, and you've got them sabotaging the school."

"Sabotage? Did I ever say sabotage?"

Kandi pointed at her watch. "Twenty-seven minutes and fifteen seconds."

"We'll make it, bunny boo," Justin said, as if talking to a baby.

Lester and Mr. Leafblad looked up, hearing the muffler of a car rattle with acceleration. "Did you hear that?" Lester asked Leafblad. He could have sworn he saw the name "Kandi" on the rear window of a car leaving the lot.

"I think they were just turning around in the parking lot. One more box, and we're finished. Thanks for providing the truck."

Lester wiped the sweat off his forehead with the sleeve of his flannel shirt. "No problem, boss."

"Did you turn off the lights?"

"Yep."

"Here's your keys," Leafblad said tossing the keys of Lester's Paleolithic pick-up. "You go ahead. I'll give the place a once-over, and I'll meet you out front."

"Thanks. I'll see you in a few minutes."

Clipper was so excited he couldn't wait to make the first stop of his Saturday night excursion. Felix, who had no idea about the kidnapping plans, had graciously given Clipper his address.

Now Clipper questioned his own motives. *Am I doing this just because it's cool? Yeah. Right. Like it would be really cool to bring a forty-three-year-old guy to a concert. Scratch that one off the list.* Was he just doing it to bend the rules a little? But there weren't any rules about who he should bring. Scratch that one off as well. So could it possibly be that he knew a guy who really didn't have any friends and wanted to make him feel a part of something? Could it be that he really cared for Felix, not out of pity, but as a friend? *There you have it,* he thought. *This is very right. Plus, it'll be a gas to see how he'll react to the whole thing.*

Felix LaBlac lived several miles away from Summit in a small wooden frame house next door to his parents. They were transplants from Eunice, Louisiana. This accounted for Felix's Cajun accent and his love of the New Orleans Saints and spicy food (he always carried a bottle of Tabasco® sauce with him). His family had moved to Indianapolis years ago. With only a fourth grade education, few people gave him much chance of finding a job because of his learning disability. But he had fooled all the naysayers, thoroughly enjoying his job as school custodian.

Felix survived the rigors of adulthood, though he remained very childlike. He had few friends and tended to worry about his ability to care for his aging parents.

As Clipper knocked on the door in a neighborhood where he had never been, he felt a bit nervous. The sounds of "Tom and Jerry" filtering out of the home reassured him and calmed his nerves. He knew Felix loved cartoons.

A few seconds after the knock, Felix peered through the front window, obviously startled when he saw Clipper. No student had ever visited him at home. Felix scurried to the door.

"Well now! I declare. Is that Clipper? My soul!"

"Hey, Felix. How's it goin'?" Clipper asked.

"What you doin', boy?"

"I know this sounds crazy, but I wanted to invite you to a concert at my church. It's a youth rock concert."

Felix stared back with a mixture of shock and enthusiasm on his face. "What you say there, Clipper, my friend? When is it? I'll be glad to come, I will."

"It's in about an hour. I'm going to kidnap a few friends of mine."

"Now hold on there, my friend, Clipper. That's not good. No, not at all. Oweeee! You done gonna get youself arrested, boy. Don't do that, now."

Clipper couldn't help laughing. Felix took the whole kidnapping thing seriously. "You don't understand, Felix. I'm just inviting people on the spur of the moment. I'm not really kidnapping."

"So you goin' kidnappin' for fun?" Felix asked.

"Right, right. Just for fun. Wanna come?" Clipper said.

"Oh me. Let's see here. Gotta think hard about this one, I do. Hmmm." He thought for what must have been all of three seconds. "Sure, I will. That sounds like a good idea, my friend."

So they began their journey, picking up a load of unsuspecting students, most of them freshmen and junior high students. Felix drew lots of strange looks, but the students soon welcomed him. He blossomed more and more at each stop. At every house, Felix took on the role of assuring the parents, as best he could. "This ain't no real kidnappin', no. This is just for fun. We be back real soon, my good friend. That's the truth," Felix would say to the parents. Every now and then in the van, Felix would squeal over the blaring Newsboys cassette, "Ooooweee! That's some rock 'n roll there!"

When they arrived at the church, students piled out of Clipper's van like clowns out of a Volkswagen. They just kept on coming, with Felix leading the pack. He reveled in the excitement of the rally. His life had been filled with little more than ammonia, mops, dust brooms, and the Cartoon Network. He felt young again, like he finally had the chance to experience the life he'd been denied during his own teen years. Some students shook their heads, embarrassed that he was even there. But most saw him as a highlight to the evening.

The students crammed into the auditorium. Huge column speakers and hulking subwoofers filled the stage. That much equipment in a space that small would seem overkill to those over twenty, like killing a mosquito with a bazooka. But the students couldn't wait. Fog machines blew out a billow of mist as the house lights faded and stage lights added a blue-green ambiance to the stage. The music started, and the band played for an hour to the delight of the students and to the horror of a few blue-haired ladies who'd agreed to come as sponsors.

Felix loved it! He danced up and down the aisles to the roar of the celebrative crowd. At one point in the concert, the students down front formed a mosh pit and there on top of the crowd Felix floated on his back as the students passed him around. A forty-three-year-old man in the mosh! No one could believe it. Felix turned from wallflower to celebrity in one night.

Justin yelled over the music at Clipper, "I can't believe it, man. You were right. Great idea! I'd never guess Felix would be such a big deal!"

"I just had a gut feeling," Clipper yelled back.

The crowd watched in amazement. The concert slowly transformed from a rock celebration to a time of worship. The band, "The Big News," had a passion for teaching Christians that worship wasn't boring. To them, worship meant a total mind, body, and soul activity, not just for the leaders, but for everyone present.

The bass guitarist told the group about his conversion the year before. He had lived on the edge of disaster for years. That past spring, he found himself in a hospital fighting an extreme addiction to alcohol and heroin. That was when he decided there had to be more to life than the drug scene. "I found Someone who knew everything about me and loved me anyway. That was when my life really began."

After the band played and sang once again and the students worshiped, a student named Troy spoke. Troy had found out two months before that he had AIDS. The auditorium that just minutes ago vibrated with the tumultuous sound of high octane Christian rock music became totally quiet.

"I thought I had it all. I had popularity. I became an all-state guard at Summit. I had center court seats to all the Pacers' home games, but I still felt empty. The kind of emptiness that you can't really feel until you slow down and think about it. Then something terrible happened. Terrible and yet I thank God for it. I found out that I had AIDS. It made me come to the reality that I wasn't invincible. I had a life. But I couldn't ignore it. I also had a time to die, and it sure seemed a whole lot closer now than it ever had.

"At first I was just really hacked off. I blamed God and I blamed anyone who had anything to do with God. I thought he was like an ogre trying to take my life. But now I realize that my choices are the reason I'm what I am today. My life may be brief; but life for everyone is. I've made a commitment to live life to the fullest from here on out. Maybe a month . . . Maybe two years . . . But I'm going to make it a celebration."

Several students in the room wiped tears from their eyes—tears of shared sympathy and sorrow. Troy stopped. He became emotional when he saw how the audience reacted. He couldn't speak for a moment, but no one moved. After he gained his composure, he continued. "I've done lots of things I regret. I wish I would have listened to some of my friends who told me to slow down and take care of myself, spiritually I mean . . . there were two guys who tried to tell me about Christ, but I just laughed them off as fanatics. Both of them are here." He cut his eyes over at Justin then went on. "I just want you to know that I've stared death in the face. At first, it scared me. I didn't know if heaven or hell existed. I didn't know what kind of pain I would have to endure. The friends I partied with, and got smashed with every weekend, avoided me like the plague, and that really hurt. I guess because they didn't have any answers either.

"But when I announced that I had AIDS, the people I had written off were the first ones that came to support me. I guess I just want to say . . ." Troy's emotions surfaced again as he paused and took a trembling breath, "thanks for that. Thanks for caring for someone who didn't deserve to be cared for."

He looked over at the band leader, who also had tears freely rolling down his face. "Guess I'm done. Thanks."

The students sat stunned and emotional. Felix buried his head in his hands and wept silently. A student who stood in the very back of the auditorium began to clap and the applause built for several seconds. One student stood, then two more, then everyone. The ovation lasted for over a minute.

After these emotional moments had passed, Shawn, the youth minister, challenged the students to come down and pray for their campuses and for one another. He also invited anyone who had never accepted Christ to come forward and take a stand at that very moment. Very few students remained in their places. Some gathered around Troy. Others came down alone and prayed. Some went to their youth ministers. Clipper and Justin were praying together for a member of the basketball team who had never accepted Christ. Kandi prayed quietly for her alcoholic father, whom she hadn't heard from in months, and for her mom, who was still a little wary about her decision to follow Christ that she'd made a month ago.

Clipper looked up from his prayer and grabbed Justin's shoulder.

Justin looked at Clipper. "What's going on?" Justin asked.

Clipper gulped and then pointed to the front. "Look!" he said, pointing to the front of the center aisle. Felix LeBlac, the 220-pound, 6-foot-3-inch custodian was weeping as Shawn shared Christ with him. The boys quietly watched as the two men prayed.

After all the other kids had been dropped off, the headlights of Clipper's van flooded the darkness of the road that led
to Felix's house. Felix talked nonstop about all that had happened, about how young he felt, even more than that, he said
he felt new. "Dis been some night. Shooweee! Da greatest night
'o my life. Tanks, Clipper. You a friend. A friend like no other,"
he said to Clipper, his eyes glistening with tears as they pulled
into Felix's neighborhood. Felix went from all smiles to an
almost stark seriousness. "Ain't nobody cared fo' me like you
done. Ain't nobody. Exceptin' Mama and Daddy."

Clipper smiled warmly. "Hey, that's what friends are for."

"Guess I ain't never had no friend like you," Felix said.

"That's what we are—friends."

"My granpaw used to sing a song long time ago. He sang—

'What a friend we have in Jesus

All our sins an' griefs to bear

What a privilege to carry
Everything to God in prayer.'
"I didn't know what that mean 'til tonight. Don't know what all that mean yet. All's I knows is that I feel clean deep down."

Clipper smiled and said, "Well, that's what Jesus does when you give your life to him. He makes you clean. Doesn't matter who you are or what you've done. Just like Troy said. He takes you, no matter what."

"Lock, stock, and barrel, huh?"

"Right, Felix. Lock, stock, and barrel."

"You know, Clipper. Tuesday is my special day."

"Your special day?"

"My birthday."

"Well, how about that."

"Forty-three-year-old man, I be. But like Shawn said to me this night. I just been borned again. That make this the best birt'day present anybody ever gived me. Jesus done did."

"That's right," Clipper said, biting his lower lip, fighting to hold back his emotions. Why am I becoming such an emotional slob?

"Ain't nobody care fo' me like you done," Felix said for the third time since the trip home began. "Ain't nobody."

As they slowed down and came to a stop in front of Felix's matchbox house, Felix continued to talk. He was like a little child. Clipper suspected Felix had looked for someone to listen to him, but always encountered people he thought were smarter than himself.

"Well, I'd better hit the road or this van's gonna turn into a pumpkin," Clipper said with a smile. Felix burst out laughing, enjoying the reference to a favorite Disney classic. "Hope you can make it, Sunday," Clipper said, reminding him of church as he wondered how his church would receive a guy like Felix.

As he drove back home, he experienced the elation known only by those who do the ordinary to receive the extraordinary. He realized he had been a critical part of God's plan to bring Felix to Jesus. And not only Felix. Two junior high students he brought to the concert also accepted Christ as Savior. As he drove back to his home, he imagined seeing the faces of these friends in heaven. He felt another rush of emotion. That night Clipper saw the world as Christ sees the world. He saw people lost and dying. He saw their hurts, fears, frustrations, and hopelessness. He saw them and he felt an intense, overwhelming desire for them to be redeemed. He imagined just a touch of the intense energy that the apostle Peter must have felt when he preached to the throngs at Pentecost. The world looked different that night. Full of desperation. Full of opportunity.

Late Sunday afternoon, Ms. Annette Jarvis, the principal of Summit High School for ten years, pulled into the school parking lot in her Lincoln Continental. She struggled to remove a large box of paperwork from the passenger side, then kicked the door closed. She looked around, hoping no one had seen her struggle.

Ms. Jarvis had the demeanor of a general. At fifty-five, she had never married. Instead, she poured her life into her career as an educator. Her strict faculty dress code elicited grumbling from teachers. But no one grumbled about her capacity as an administrator at Summit High. She put in more hours than anyone else.

When she unlocked and opened the door to the school, she was suspicious. There was no high pitched beep warning her that she had a minute to disengage the alarm with the numeric keypad.

"Felix!" She whispered under her breath to herself. Her momentary suspicions evaporated at the thought of her custodian. In all probability he had forgotten to engage the alarm when he left Friday night after work. Now because of his inefficiency, she would have to do a complete walk-through to assure that all was well despite the alarm oversight.

After opening her office and dropping off the box of documents, she took a stroll through the facilities.

Her high heels echoed down the dark empty hallways. She did a quick inspection of the classrooms, using a flashlight rather than turning on each light. The west hall checked out fine, with the exception of finger prints smudging some of the glass dividers. "Felix, Felix." She muttered under her breath, agitated with the absent-minded janitor. She had inherited him when she came to the school and had hoped from the start that he would move on to something else. She rarely affirmed Felix, hoping her negativity would be an added motivation for him to leave.

She moved along to the center hallway, which included the counselor's office and the library. As she walked, she continued her mental critique of Felix's performance. Finally she went down the east hall, which housed the computer rooms and the science labs. She swung the flashlight's beam across the science lab with its ancient faucets, flasks, and jars. Everything appeared to be in working order, even clean.

Then she went to the Computer Lab.

As she walked toward the lab, her heart began to race as she saw a scene unmatched in her thirty-two years in the field of secondary education. Her shoes crunched on broken glass from the shattered observation window. She pointed the flashlight to the back wall of the lab and glared at the spray painted words that covered the walls—"Western High Rules!!"

She felt dizzy as she guided the light across the wall and saw a second spray of graffiti, smaller, yet more vulgar. Several large rectangular ceiling tiles had been stripped, leaving air ducts and computer cables exposed. Beer cans were strewn across the floor, leaving small puddles of the stale liquid and a stench that made the suburban classroom smell like a sleazy back alley bar.

It took Ms. Jarvis a few moments to digest the damage and the disgust of the scene before she realized the computer lab had no computers. She collapsed into the first chair she could find and buried her head in her hands.

This wasn't just a cruel case of vandalism by a rival school. It was burglary, to the tune of sixty thousand dollars.

Justin tried to keep his panic to a minimum. During the past couple of months, he had funneled most of his energy into basketball. He had stepped into a starting roll as guard just in time for the play-offs. Summit High did well in the dark horse role making it to state tournament and even into the final eight. But when Justin finally woke up from his hoop dreams, he found he was into the final weeks of the semester with a ton of projects and papers due. Now the final school assignments were due within days. He wished teachers gave extra credit for free throws, but, alas, they demanded the real deal. Jocks didn't get special privileges at Summit.

So it was late and Justin found himself pounding away at his Mac, trying to make sense out of a research paper on the Lincoln assassination. He would type, stare blankly at the screen, take a few sips of Dr. Pepper, and continue on while half listening to the news update that was delayed by a late game that evening. The newscaster droned on about the top stories—Pacers play-off hopes and a recent string of murders in the downtown area. During one of those moments where the computer screen seemed to be sucking the intelligence out of his brain as he stared at it, his ears perked up. *Did I hear what I think I heard?* he thought. He heard the words *Summit High School*, and they didn't come from the sports reporter.

"Hey, Justin! You ought to come in here. Something happened last night at Summit High," his dad called out to him.

"What?"

"Don't know. They said the story's coming up."

After an onslaught of used car, mattress, and tire commercials, footage of Summit appeared on the screen. The anchor from the local CBS affiliate began, "Apparently school rivalry and vandalism continue to be partners in crime. Police officials report a rival school burglarized and vandalized Summit High School. Roughly sixty thousand dollars' worth of new school computers were lifted from Summit's refurbished computer lab. It happened sometime between 6 P.M. Friday night and 9 A.M. Sunday morning. Although the police have speculated from markings left at the scene that the crimes were committed by students from another school, they wouldn't release the identity of the school in question." The camera then focused on a visibly distraught Ms. Jarvis. "Ms. Annette Jarvis, principal at Summit High, used the opportunity to plea for more funding in school security."

Ms. Jarvis spoke tentatively, yet with emotion to the reporter. "We just spent a massive amount of money to secure this equipment, but why make these purchases if we can't protect ourselves from this kind of thing? It's discouraging, very discouraging."

Following the short sound bite, the reporter continued. "Evidently someone disengaged the security alarm system and the crime scene remained undiscovered until this afternoon."

"Wow!" Justin's dad remarked. "Bet some Western High students did it."

Justin didn't say a word as he walked slowly back to the study, trying to digest the incident, along with what he and the others had seen Friday night. He stood in a dazed stupor, reviewing each detail of what they had seen that night, trying as hard as he could to discount the two events as totally unrelated.

He remembered how Lester had moved with determination even though the boxes were obviously heavy.

Could the boxes have been large enough to hold computers? He even remembered thinking they might be computer boxes. *Would Leafblad have vandalized too? He had worked hard to help raise the funds to buy the computers. Why would he steal them? Maybe he just forgot to reset the alarm after he left. That has to be it,* he thought. *Dad's right. It's Western High. They're just feeling cocky from winning state again. That's about as low as it gets.*

He wanted to believe that Lester and Leafblad had nothing to do with the whole thing other than maybe forgetting to reset the alarm. But somehow even he couldn't swallow his theory.

The phone rang. Kandi's voice was tight with excitement. "Justin, I saw something just now that you won't believe."

"I saw it too, Kandi," Justin interjected.

"What do you think?" Kandi asked.

"I think they did it," Justin said quietly.

"Maybe Leafblad just forgot to reset the alarm," Kandi suggested. "I mean, do you really think that he'd tear the place apart? I could see Lester doing something like that, but a teacher—"

"What if they set the whole thing up, Kandi? They could have done it to throw off the police."

"So what are we going to do?" Kandi asked.

"We've got to tell what we know."

"Justin, let's think about this first."

"What's there to think about?" Justin argued.

"If Leafblad's really involved, which we don't know for sure—"

"We've got a pretty good idea that—"

"But if he isn't," Kandi continued, "we're accusing an innocent teacher. I like him. Plus, I've got a class with him and—"

"OK, OK, I see your point. Let's just stay cool about the whole thing for now. But if this thing is what we think it is, we're the only witnesses."

"We don't know that," Kandi said. "Somebody else could have seen them. In fact, I'm sure that someone did. Had to."

"It was dark and—" Justin continued.

"But they had to do something with the computers. Plus, they would have to make at least three trips to the school in order to get everything in that old truck." Kandi struggled to defend her position.

Justin continued. "Don't you see? He just happened to hit his lights out of habit, and he turned them off as quickly as they came on. They didn't want to be seen."

Justin heard a click from call waiting. "Can you hold on for a sec?"

"There's something really sick about call waiting. Go ahead," Kandi said.

"Hello."

Clipper started right in. "You won't believe what I saw on the—"

"Been there. Saw it. Old news," Justin said.

"So what do you think?" Clipper asked.

"I don't know what to think about it."

"I think they did it," Clipper said.

"I wish we had never stopped," Justin said with regret.

"You're the one, man. 'Oh, come on . . . please.' You were beggin' her to stop." Clipper took a breath and then continued. "So, when do we all go?"

"Where?" Justin asked.

Clipper acted surprised that Justin didn't follow him. "Duh! When do we go tell Ms. Jarvis what we saw?"

"I don't think it's as simple as that."

"What!?" Clipper was incredulous.

"Think it through, think it through. Look at all the possible scenarios. We speak up now, and we add ourselves to the list of suspects."

"But we're our own alibi," Clipper protested.

"So was the Manson family. Listen, Kandi's on the other line."

"But—"

"We'll talk tomorrow."

"You really *are* in love, aren't you? It starts . . . you think you know a guy."

"Bye," Justin said.

"I feel so . . . alone . . ." Clipper said with a phony, melo-dramatic whine.

"Sleep tight." Justin clicked the phone to return to Kandi. "Hey, Babe?"

"You have no idea how much I hate being on hold."

"I think you've told me that a few times."

Click. The call waiting alert came forth once again but this time on Kandi's side.

"You know if you take that, you're a hypocrite," Justin said with a laugh.

Kandi giggled and pressed the button on the phone. "Hello."

"Hey, girl. It's Autumn. Did you hear what I heard?"

"I did."

"I think we all need to have a long talk before we say any-thing about what we saw Friday night," Autumn said.

"I agree."

"It's like *The Firm* without Tom Cruise."

"But, hey, we've got Clipper Hayes," Kandi said. They both laughed.

"Do you think they saw us?" Kandi asked.

"No, I don't. They may have heard the muffler, but I don't think they could have gotten a very good look. They were too busy ripping off computers, one of which, by the way, contains three book summaries for my honors English class."

"Ouch," Kandi said with sympathy. "What are you going to do?"

"Don't know. I've got an older version on a floppy."

"I'm sorry."

"That's the least of my worries. You know, we could just leave this whole thing up to the cops," Autumn suggested.

"You going to tell your folks?"

"Not yet."

"I've got Justin on call waiting."

"Why am I not surprised?" Autumn said.

"I'll see you tomorrow. I'll pick you up around 7:30?" Kandi proposed.

"That'll be great. See ya."

She clicked back to Justin. "I'm back."

"OK. Let me guess. Autumn?" Justin asked Kandi.

"Righto."

"What did she think? She's got more brains than all of us."

"She said we should wait awhile before we say anything."

"Look, maybe I'll just tell what I saw," Justin said, his conscience tugging at him.

"But we were in my car. Plus you'd be lying if you said you were alone," Kandi pointed out. "If you're going to tell it, let's tell the whole truth. But please, let's just wait."

Another click interrupted them.

"Is that my call waiting or yours?" Kandi asked.

"Mine," Justin said.

"I'll marry you if you ignore it," Kandi said with a twinge of flirtation.

"A man's gotta do what a man's gotta do." Justin tapped the line button.

A strange voice was on the other end of the line. "Hi, this is Long Distance Communications. Are you pleased with the service you've been receiving from your current long-distance company?"

"Yep."

"But what if I told you I could save you—"

Justin smiled and interrupted the sales pitch. "I'd tell you I'm busy. See ya."

Click.

"Wow, you're quick!"

"Can you believe we get sales calls on a Sunday night? Listen, why don't we just get together at lunch tomorrow and decide what we're going to do. This 'call waiting' business is about to drive me batty. We need to pray about this before we do anything and take a long hard look at the worst case scenario, and make sure we're prepared for the worst. If this is as funky as we think it is, we need to be prepared for . . . anything and everything."

"You're making me nervous, Justin."

"Sorry."

"All right, sweety. I like you, bye."

"I really, really like you too," Justin said. He smiled as he hung up, remembering the promise they made a week ago that the word *love* was too high octane for their relationship. So they just affirmed each other with the word *like*.

Justin's father walked into his son's bedroom. "Sounds like some pretty heavy duty conversation, son. Everything OK?"

"Hi, Dad. Yeah, just great. We were just talking about the robbery at the school."

Mr. Henderson sat down on the side of Justin's bed. "Any idea who might have done such an awful thing?"

"We've got some guesses." Justin stopped and looked at his father. They sat silent for a moment.

His father took a deep breath and said, "You want to share that with me?"

"No, Dad," Justin said hesitantly. "Not right now. I need you to trust me."

Looking around the poster-filled room, Mr. Henderson's eyes settled on a picture of Justin with Reggie White, made when the NFL player had spoken at an FCA meeting. He looked back at his son. "Is this going to affect any of your classes?"

"Probably half of them, Dad. But please trust me. I won't do anything wrong."

Placing a hand on Justin's shoulder, Mr. Henderson squeezed it slightly. "Let me know what I can do, Justin. I'm here if you need me."

"Thanks, Dad."

Justin whispered a prayer of thanksgiving for a dad who was available but rarely nosed into his business. It was as if God lessened the pain of being abandoned by his mother by giving him a truly super dad. *Trust* was a major word in their home, perhaps because the past contained so much broken trust. As Justin's dad walked back into the living room, Justin took a deep breath, shook his head, and dove back into 1865 and the Ford Theater.

As the students scurried in from a Monday morning cloud-burst, they traded rumors and speculation about the burglary. In the eyes of most Summit High students, Western High rivals were the prime suspects. School personnel had tried to paint over the markings, but even three coats didn't make the words illegible. No more than ten minutes after the first bell rang, several student factions were planning retaliation by stealing and torturing the mascot or slashing the tires of Western's athletic bus. They were like hungry sharks who'd just caught the fresh scent of blood.

"Can you believe it?" Clipper asked Justin as they walked in from outside. Clipper carried a long flat box. "These guys are out for blood. They want Western bad. I think that's even more of a reason to let Jarvis know what we saw."

"Have you ever talked to her?" Justin said.

"Are you kidding? I don't think she even knows I exist," Clipper laughed.

"I've been in meetings with her, and I think I can say for a fact she doesn't trust anyone under the age of eighteen," Justin said ruefully.

"She's not supposed to trust us, Justin."

"But I still think we've got to talk to her," Justin added, realizing he contradicted himself every time he opened his mouth.

"When?"

"I don't know. Maybe this afternoon."

"That's too soon for me." Clipper also flip-flopped from one way of thinking to the next and back again.

"What?" Justin asked in surprise.

"It's all going too fast. This is big-time stuff! Plus, we promised Kandi and Autumn we'd do it together."

"It might be better if we leave the girls out of this whole thing," Justin proposed. Then he looked at the box. "Uh . . . what's with the box?"

Clipper looked down at the box he held at waist level, as if he had forgotten what he held. He paused a moment, then brightened. "Oh, I didn't tell you? Guess with all the stuff that's happening I forgot to invite you. I'm organizing a surprise birthday party for Felix."

"When's his birthday?"

"Today."

"Cool."

Clipper looked up and down the hall, then opened up the box to show him the large sheet cake that his mom had baked for the occasion. "We're going to surprise him after school today."

Being around her friends had lessened Kandi's fears about what she had seen Friday night. She wanted to forget the whole situation, at least temporarily. She worried about third period when she went to Leafblad's class. She could just imagine Leafblad calling her to the front and asking her to talk to him after class in private. She had visions of bribes, lies, abuse, and threats. After all, the car literally had her name plastered on it. She hardly looked at Leafblad the entire period. To her relief, such an encounter never occurred.

After lunch she went to her locker to prepare for fourth period as she pondered what might happen next. Lester came up behind her. She almost jumped out of her skin when he tapped her on the shoulder.

"Oops. Didn't mean to scare you, Kandi," he said with a smirk.

Kandi stood there, stunned. She couldn't even produce her "positive school persona."

Lester didn't wait for a response. "I hear you got your driver's license Friday. My congrats. What is that thing you were driving? A blue Sable? Kinda old. Sounds like it needs a new muffler. Let me know if you need to have that fixed. I have a friend whose dad owns an auto repair shop. He could fix you up, no problem."

Still Kandi said nothing.

Lester continued. "Who shoe-polished your name on the car?"

Kandi's heart pounded as she tried to mask her nervousness. "Don't know. I just . . . Well, I saw that for the first time Friday afternoon."

"I bet Justin did it," Lester said smiling coolly and leaning up against the locker. He stood only about eighteen inches from her face and his cigarette breath made her want to gag. Her fingers tingled. Lester wasn't a large guy, but he could intimidate. His parents were well-off, but he definitely had the grunge look, complete with an old army jacket and baggy jeans. His hair fell into his eyes, and he hadn't shaved in several days.

"I've got to go, Lester," Kandi said as she turned away.

"Wait a second, Kandi," he said firmly, grabbing her arm.

Kandi could no longer hide her nervousness. She hated it when a guy grabbed her arm like that. Mostly because it reminded her of her drunken father's behavior. She instinctively cringed, waiting for a blow. Her eyes moistened.

"I'm not finished talking to you. That's so rude! Don't you know how rude that is for you to just walk away while someone's talking to you?" Lester said, loud enough for other students to hear.

"I'm gonna scream 'rape' if you don't let go of my arm. NOW!" Kandi insisted. Her fear bubbled to the surface.

"I wouldn't scream now," Lester said, lowering his voice to a threatening whisper. "I'll let go, but first you're going to answer a few questions. I think I saw you the other night. Friday night. You were snooping around the school while I helped Leafblad rearrange his room. I saw the word *Kandi* on your rear window. That gave it away. One tip," he smiled and then continued, "if you're going to snoop around like some kind of 'teen detective babe,' you really ought to keep a lower profile." He gave her a conspiratorial wink. "Some stuff happened after we left that we didn't have anything to do with. I know you probably think otherwise, but nobody's asking for your opinion, so keep your mouth shut. I don't want to have a bad reputation, and I can sure make yours look like mud, less than mud. OK? You understand?"

Kandi didn't respond to the whispered threat.

"You don't know what a guy like me would do to protect his reputation. You don't know me, Kandi. If you just forget what you saw, you'll be fine. But never underestimate my influence around here. You think I'm just a punk. But just ask a few people. Just find out about me. If you cross me on this one, I'll send you packing!"

Kandi slipped away quickly, slamming her locker shut. As she left, Lester called out, "You were alone, weren't you?"

She hurried toward her next class. As she walked she thought to herself, *Why did Justin insist on checking it out? Why do I always end up in these things? God, where's your protection from these people?*

Suddenly she felt another hand on her arm. She yanked her arm away and shouted, "Leave me alone!"

When she turned she found a puzzled Justin.

"What's wrong, Kandi?"

"I can't talk about it," Kandi said, turning away from him.

"Kandi, you've got to tell me! What's going on?"

"I just . . . I can't, Justin. I don't want to talk to you right now. I can't."

"We need to talk soon. I've made a decision," Justin insisted.

"I have too." Kandi gave him a hard look. "We need to just forget what we saw," Kandi countered.

"Kandi, something's up. I can tell."

Kandi started crying, and Justin put his arms around her.

"Come on over here." They broke their embrace as Justin took her hand and led her to a deserted stairwell. "I saw you walking away from Lester. Did he say something to you?"

Kandi nodded her head. "He saw my car." She became more upset. "Why did we have to do that?" she said through tears as she beat his chest softly in frustration. "He said that he'd ruin my life if I said anything."

Justin couldn't hide his anger toward Lester. "That's not going to happen, Kandi. You don't have anything to worry about."

"I'm not asking you to go into some macho thing. I don't need a knight in shining armor. I just need a guy who can keep me out of this whole mess. I want to forget the whole thing. OK?" Kandi pleaded.

"I promise. You don't have a thing to worry about. Just let me handle it," Justin said with a bit of hesitation. He knew what he had to do. Case closed. This mess smelled worse than Clipper's gym locker.

Autumn's reaction was different from Kandi's. She didn't let the concerns of what might happen bog down the activities of her day. She and Clipper were too busy planning Felix's surprise birthday party to worry about anything else. She wanted Felix to become involved with believers somehow, somewhere. When Clipper came up with the idea of the birthday party, Autumn got behind it 100 percent.

Autumn saw Felix leaving the administrative offices between classes and ran to greet him. She was so excited, she knew it would take a lot of effort not to spill the beans and tell him about their plans for him after he got off work. When Autumn caught up with him, she realized he was upset. He headed toward the supply closet, looking at a blue slip of paper.

"Hey Felix! How's it going?"

"Oh, hello there, Autumn," he said with a forced smile.

"Felix, you look upset. What's up?"

He pointed at the paper, "This is what been goin' on. Forgot to turn on the alarm system, they say. Says that's why the school got robbed the other night. I can't believe it, no. I thought for sure I did that."

"You're kidding!" Autumn replied.

"No, I ain't."

Autumn couldn't believe it either. "I'm sorry, Felix."

"They say I gots one more chance to be good. Or else they goin' let me go."

The threat of termination really infuriated Autumn. It made her even more angry at Lester and Mr. Leafblad. *Whether they stole the computers or not,* she thought, *they were responsible for the alarm not being reset.* This really made Autumn mad. She'd seen injustice before. She'd even been the victim of prejudice and injustice. She knew what it was to suffer for the rights that she enjoyed. And the injustices Felix endured were no different. She had seen him on his hands and knees cleaning the floors and thanklessly rearranging furniture and supplies. He had worked for years at this school, rarely calling in sick or asking for favors. And yet because he didn't talk or act like others, he was considered less of a person. But this injustice could be undone. She knew Felix wasn't to blame for this problem. "Don't worry about this. I have some information that will clear this whole thing up," she said.

"You do?"

Autumn smiled and said, "I can't go into it right now, but chances are you did everything you were supposed to do, but somebody else—" She realized at that point he wouldn't understand much more. "Just believe me. You're going to be fine."

She couldn't wait until later this afternoon when they would surprise Felix. She thought about all the times the administration chewed him out for forgetting things and wondered if she could somehow help him. The thought stayed with her throughout her last class.

She brainstormed possibilities. Felix needed something to help him remember all his work assignments. *A daytimer/"to-do" list type notebook? Nope, he doesn't write things down that well. A microcassette player? That's it!* she thought. *He could keep it in his pocket, record different jobs, and play it back during the day to remind him of his responsibilities.*

That settled it for her. She'd go to the office supply store after school and pick one up for him. The cost would probably be the equivalent of one night at the BurgeRama, but she didn't care. She wanted to help Felix somehow, even if it put a dent in her personal budget.

Throughout the school day, word spread until there were twenty-five students wanting to help Felix celebrate his birthday. Clipper and Autumn told everyone to meet in the school's Little Theater. The Little Theater used to be the music building until the program outgrew the space. Mrs. Martinez, the drama professor at Summit, allowed the students access to the Little Theater. She knew this party would mean a lot to Felix. She told Clipper about the many times Felix had gone the extra mile for her during performances. She agreed to help by asking Felix to mop the stage floor that afternoon. This would assure that Felix would be in the theater. Before the day ended, Mrs. Martinez had promised to make a special point to remind him.

Clipper knew Mrs. Martinez was the only teacher Felix addressed by her first name and only because she insisted. She also told Clipper that Felix was the only member of the faculty or staff she felt she could trust.

⌒H⌒

The students gathered shortly after school in the Little Theater. Autumn and Clipper had done a pretty good job of organizing a surprise party—complete with confetti, streamers, music,
cake, soft drinks, and enough M&Ms (Felix's favorite snack) to
put Indiana's entire population of preschoolers into a sugar fit.

As the friends gathered, they swapped stories that grew
longer and taller with every passing moment. Since the Youth
Rally Saturday night, Felix's reputation as the dancing Cajun
custodian had grown. They really didn't know him that well,
but each one had personal stories of encounters they'd had
with him in the past.

Debbie, a senior at Summit, told of the time she saw him
on a ladder with rag and spray cleaner washing the clock. He
misunderstood the teacher's instruction to *watch* the clock
when he came in to clean between classes.

Clipper recalled the time he and Felix got into a long philo-
sophical argument over the use of artificial turf in major league
sports. "If you don't got to pay no one to cut da grass," Felix
reasoned, "you can pay mo' money fo' de players."

But the group also recalled the small heroic acts of Felix.
The times he would stay late to lock up after fund-raising
events. He also avoided turning things into the lost and found
without first trying to find the owners of the property himself.
He loved his job, and it showed.

A student called Troy on his cell phone. "He's heading your
way, guys."

Troy relayed the message. "Hit the lights! He's on the way."

The Little Theater went almost totally black with the exception of the exit lights. Everyone found a place and got quiet. In the foyer, keys jingled and the door opened. It was hard for the students not to laugh as they heard Felix singing to himself a song he'd learned at the youth rally Saturday night: "Got da joy, joy, joy, joy, joy, joy! Got da joy, joy, joy, joy, joy, joy—two tree fo', down in my heart . . . "

He opened the main stage door. "Shooowee! This place is dark today! That Cindy done left no lights on for sure!"

Suddenly the stage lights blinded him and loud shouts of "Happy Birthday" came from everywhere. Confetti filled the air around Felix and the music began. It was like Times Square on New Year's Eve. Felix soon realized the party was for him. After years of watching parties at the school from the hallway, this celebration was his.

Felix had never felt like this before. He was so happy he thought he might surely burst from the excitement. He felt like a real important person. For one shining moment, he found himself the center of attention, and he couldn't believe it

Up until last week, his most cherished moments had been short conversations with students, a simple thank you for a job well done or a smile from someone who appreciated his strange sense of humor. But now the students he loved were honoring him. For the first time since he came to work at Summit High School, he felt like he belonged. They loved him and he loved them.

"What do you think?" Clipper asked, interrupting Felix's thoughts. "Did we get ya?"

"Whoooweee! You done got de ole Felix fo' sho!" he replied.

The students laughed and sang "Happy Birthday" as Kandi came out in a sparkling purple top hat she had borrowed from the costume closet. She carried the birthday cake filled with forty-three candles.

The light of the candles danced across her face, her sparkling brown eyes, and white teeth. Justin eyed her admiringly. She had never looked so beautiful and cheerful as she did at that moment, he thought. He remembered the shy Kandi he had met just two months ago. He found it hard to believe how much she had changed since they first met.

He had grown to admire her not only as an attractive, athletic young woman but even more as a survivor. She'd been through so much before she came to Summit, and even more in the past two months. Yet she triumphed unbelievably and he liked that. When she looked at him during the off-key version of "Happy Birthday," it was as if they had a conversation of glances. They looked at each other and smiled. Justin shook his head ever so slightly and raised his eyebrows. She winked back at him, innocently, playfully.

After the song, several students called for a speech. It was more than Felix could take, more than he had ever imagined possible for his life. His chin quivered and a tear dropped from his cheek; he wiped it on his sleeve. The celebrative noise came to a quiet hush as Felix prepared to put a few words together.

"I ain't much for speakin', no. This has been de greatest moment of ole Felix's life. You know I ain't smart, not smart like you. But this ole boy got some love in his heart for you, yeah, some big kind o' love for you. You here are the greatest people I knows." The tears now rolled off his face one after another.

Clipper could no longer fight the quiver of his own chin. This wasn't his idea of a party, but some things just happen.

Felix continued, "But the greatest thing you done for me, was what you done by showin' me who Jesus is. He ain't just a word to say when you get mad. And I learned to say it the right way." Felix collected his thoughts and he said slowly, "He is my Savior and my Lord."

The room became quiet. Some were stunned by his words. Not everyone in the room claimed what Felix claimed, and they were stunned. Finally, applause rose from the room, and Felix turned his back to blow his nose. He didn't seem to know how to act or what to say.

Then Autumn took charge. "We aren't finished, Felix. What's a birthday party without gifts?"

The basketball team had pooled their money and bought Felix a New Orleans Saints sweatshirt. He got a baseball shirt, basketball jersey, and a football sweatshirt begged from the school's coaches. Finally, Autumn pulled the microcassette player out of a white paper bag.

"Sorry, I didn't have time to wrap it," she said.

"My, my! What is it for?" Felix was awed by the small machine.

"It's a microcassette tape player for your job."

"My job? Shoooweee! What I do with it at my work?"

"Simple, Felix. You know how you're always worried about forgetting things? This will help. Just make a verbal note."

"What you talkin' bout there . . . a verbal note."

"Just like this." Autumn popped a cassette in with a message she had already recorded. The recorder played the message, "Don't forget to wash the clock and that Summit High loves you!" Everyone laughed and applauded.

Other gifts were given. Some simple, others comical, but Felix treated them all as if they were fifth-generation heirlooms. Even the whoopee cushion! No one was sure if he understood its purpose, but he showed unending and sincere gratitude for it nonetheless.

And last, Clipper pulled out the new leather Bible that Justin, Kandi, and several other students pitched in to buy him. Felix's eyes widened as he opened the hard cardboard box, which held the beautiful blue Bible. The leather aroma wafted its way up as Felix stood, stunned by the generosity of his friends. Through tears, he saw his name embossed in finely crafted script on the front cover. His hands trembled ever so slightly as he took the Bible out of its box and quietly said, "Thank you."

The party went from touching to hilarious as Felix demonstrated the moves he had premiered at the concert Saturday night. Sounds from the latest Newsboys CD filled the theater as the group partied.

After the party, Justin and Kandi walked slowly to Justin's '79 Caprice Classic in the back student parking lot. The May sky produced one of its classic Indiana sunsets. All the worries and cares about the computer scandal seemed to dissolve under the delicate sky of pastel orange and purple.

"I gotta tell you, Justin. You scare me," Kandi said.

"What?" Justin said, alarmed.

"Well, you do. Every guy who I've felt like this about usually ends up ripping my heart out and tearing it into tiny shreds," she explained. "But you're different."

They both laughed nervously.

Justin stopped walking and took her hand casually, looking her in the eyes. "I'm pretty freaked out about it too. I mean, we thought from the beginning that we'd pal around with friends a lot and date a little. Right?"

Kandi nodded as Justin continued, "But I don't want to date anybody else. It would be weird if I did. I'd just be thinking about you."

"You're so cute it's almost sickening," she said laughing.

"Thanks a lot, Shweety," he said with his best Bogart lisp.

"Would you cut it out?"

"You started it!"

Laughing, they found their faces just a few inches from each other. The laughter died as they became aware of sudden intimacy. Slowly, seriously they looked into each other's eyes.

"OK, guys!" Clipper yelled as he walked up. "Hold it right there!" he shouted like the captain of the purity patrol. "I tell ya, I can't leave you two alone for two minutes without it turning into some kind of Sandra Bullock moment."

"You wait, Clipper. You just wait," Justin said as he shook his finger back and forth like a second-grade teacher. Kandi laughed with embarrassment as she buried her forehead in Justin's collarbone.

Kandi tried to avoid Lester the next morning, but he headed directly for her locker. She regretted turning down Justin's offer to walk her to her class. She had told Justin, "I may be a little paranoid, but I'm not a preschooler."

And now Lester was walking toward her with an obvious agenda. The scowl on his face and even the way he walked left little doubt that he was beyond angry.

"You did it," Lester accused.

"Did what?"

"I don't have time for the innocent act."

"Lester, get out. I didn't do anything."

"You went to Jarvis."

"Jarvis? No way." Kandi shook her head firmly, her eyes wide and scared.

"Then why did I get this?" he held out a wrinkled slip of paper. The note read:

To: Lester McCord
From: Ms. Jarvis
Please see me immediately after your last class for a brief
meeting.

"I know why I got this. I've only been called into her office a couple of times. And I can promise you that it's not for a student of the month award. I can't believe you'd tell. I gave you fair warning."

Kandi sputtered, "I didn't tell anybody anything. Have you ever thought that I might not be the only one who saw you out there? Did that ever enter your mind?"

"I don't know about everybody, Kandi. I just saw you and your car."

"This is not about me, Lester," Kandi said louder.

"I don't really give a flyin' leap. I just want you to know that whoever went to Ms. Jarvis must not care about your well-being because you're in way over your head. You know what I mean? It's not just my word against yours. I've got an ace in the hole. So you and whoever need to back way off, or I'll wow you with my influence around this place. You have no idea what I can do to girls like you with just a phone call."

Kandi stood in stunned disbelief as he freely railed accusations, threats, and vulgarities with unending malice. At that point, Kandi could listen no more. She just wanted to get as far away from him as fast as she could. Without warning him, she walked away.

"Kandi," he raised his voice as she moved away from him. "I'd get your bags packed because if this thing goes down like

I think it will, you'll be going back to Texas with or without your sweet mommy." Lester's voice changed into a deep cowboy drawl and increased in volume enough to turn more than a few heads. "Headin' back to Texas to see yer old drunk daddy! Yee-haw."

She felt so angry she could have leveled him on the spot. Instead, she decided to have a chat with Justin. She could expect Lester to be Lester. But Justin! What was he thinking? Could he have really gone to Jarvis without consulting her first? Could he have left her exposed to the shenanigans of this creep? She prayed her instincts were wrong. She prayed Justin said nothing and that Lester got called to Ms. Jarvis' office for some other minor school offense. After all, he wasn't a model student. He could be called in every day of the year if the school had the administrative support to handle it.

Kandi stormed across campus looking for Justin and finally found him talking with his history teacher, Mrs. Tyndale. The teacher saw Kandi behind Justin and stopped midsentence. "Uh, Justin, I think somebody wants to talk to you," she said half smiling.

"Oh, hi, Kandi," Justin said innocently.

Kandi pulled him out of the hallway traffic into a hallway corner. "What's up?" he asked calmly but with some reserve.

Kandi just bore a hole through him with her angry stare.

"Uh-oh," he said. "Did Lester talk to you?"

Kandi shot back, "Did Lester talk to me? Is that the question?" she asked angrily and then louder, "Did Lester talk to me?"

Justin winced and Kandi continued, "Yeah . . . uh huh . . . he talked to me all right. He certainly didn't send me flowers.

I thought we agreed to lay low for a while. I don't know. Call me crazy, but I thought you'd at least consult me before you did something as stupid as—"

Justin matched her intensity. "I went to Ms. Jarvis to protect you from all this!"

"Protect me? Did you say *protect me*? Well, why don't you just leave me in a room full of snakes next time you want to make me feel protected."

Students stopped to watch as the confrontation grew louder. "Would you just settle down. Let's talk about what I did and what I didn't do," Justin said in a soft but persistent voice. "I'm keeping you out of this. I'm not going to even mention you. It's me and Lester."

Kandi interrupted his list of declarations. "You don't get it, do you? It doesn't matter if I'm involved or not. He's going after me, period, no matter who talks."

"If he did anything to you, if he touched you, he'll regret it. He's full of hot air," Justin said.

"Well, I'm getting a *tad* wind burned," Kandi said furiously.

"Lester will know that this has nothing to do with you after our meeting today."

"Hello-oo," Kandi said poking his chest with her finger. "Don't you understand? It doesn't matter whether its me or not. I'm his scapegoat. I'm his bargaining chip. The gun is at my head. Everybody knows you. They grew up with you. It would take a lot of work to damage your reputation. But me? No one knows me. I'm *easy* to destroy. Plus, he knows that if he really wants to get to you, he threatens me. Are you up to speed yet?" Kandi finished sarcastically.

Justin grew quiet. Kandi's argument made sense. He paused and Kandi did too.

The truth rushed in on him. "OK, you're right. If he wanted to get to me, threatening you would do it." Justin thought carefully about what to say next. He had already asked to meet with Ms. Jarvis and Lester about the incident. Should he ask her to forget the meeting? Would she even go for that? Setting up a meeting about a major robbery, then asking to be excused would certainly leave a lot of unanswered questions in Ms. Jarvis' mind. But he did have excellent rapport with Ms. Jarvis. The more he thought about it, the more he became convinced he had handled the situation poorly. He should have at least told Kandi about his plans to talk to the principal.

He took a deep breath. "What can I do?" he asked sheepishly.

"You can cancel the meeting," Kandi replied flatly.

Justin looked away. "OK. I'll cancel . . . for today. But we need to talk about this some more. For better or worse, we saw what we saw."

"I agree. We'll talk."

Justin turned and walked away as the tardy bell rang. Kandi called out, "Justin?" He turned around. Kandi walked over and kissed his cheek and whispered, "Thanks."

All morning Kandi's thoughts raced. She replayed the asinine threats that Lester hurled at her before school. *He thinks he's the Godfather of Summit High*. It really burned her. She had to do something.

Kandi needed space. She needed some time away from everyone, so she skipped lunch to find a quiet place to think, pray, and try to make some sense out of the whole situation.

She walked outside to sit on the bleachers of the practice field and search for answers from her small New Testament that Justin had given her a few weeks ago. It was a modern translation that included Psalms and Proverbs.

She knew the answers could be found within the pages of that small black book. The problem was she didn't know where to look. *Lots of words,* she thought. And the beginning of Matthew was filled with all those "begats." So she just opened the Bible praying, "Lord, I don't have a clue how you speak to people like Justin and Autumn say you do. But I've only got twenty-five minutes, and I really need some kind of clue."

Kandi sat quietly, feeling a sense of peace and reassurance. She looked up at the blue sky and smiled. She was thankful she could turn to God and didn't have to depend on her own strength alone. A sweet May breeze lifted her hair, then reached the pages of the Bible. When the wind stopped, she saw that the Bible was opened to Psalm 37. There she read these words:

Stop your anger! Turn off your wrath.
Don't fret and worry—it only leads to harm.
For the wicked shall be destroyed,
But those who trust the Lord shall be given every blessing.
Only a little while and the wicked shall disappear.

Tears welled up in her eyes as she read the words in verse 12:

The Lord is laughing at those who plot against the godly,
For he knows their judgment day is coming.

"OK, God," she prayed, "I hear you. I'm ready."

10

For Justin, lunch was a nightmare. He felt shaky about Kandi. He didn't want to lose her. He shouldn't have talked to Ms. Jarvis. He should have consulted Kandi about his decision. Instead, he did the macho thing. He took the bull by both horns and said, "I'm a big boy. I can make this choice by myself." He didn't even think about the risks.

He spent the entire lunch period looking for her. He asked everyone if they'd seen her and looked pretty silly in the process. The knot in his stomach overpowered his hunger. He wanted to see her again. Not in an hour, not after school. He wanted to see her immediately! He wanted to tell her how much he wanted things to be right between them. He was evolving into a bumbling romantic, ready to shower her with flowers, and even the sticky sweet love songs that can only be heard on one totally uncool soft rock station in town. He was desperate.

Kandi finally caught up with Justin just before their last class. He looked relieved when he saw her, "Where have you been? I looked all over for you at lunch. You scared me half to death."

"I just needed some time to think about this whole thing."

"I've been thinking too. I really blew it today. I've been worried all day that you were just going to write me off. And then I didn't see you at lunch. You vanished! I put you in danger—" Justin couldn't finish his sentence.

"What could Lester do to me that he hasn't done already?"

"A whole lot."

"Justin, could you just hold on a second and listen? I'm with you. You need to do this. It's the right thing to do, no matter what the consequences are."

"Are you sure? I was just about to head for the office to apologize and tell Ms. Jarvis there wasn't a reason for the meeting," Justin explained.

"There is a reason for the meeting. You've got to let her know what you saw," Kandi said earnestly.

"I don't want you there," Justin assured her.

Kandi laughed. "Good, cuz I'm not going. Lester gives me the creeps."

When Clipper and Autumn walked up, Clipper was relieved to see Justin and Kandi smiling and talking. Although he joked about their relationship, he was really afraid the whole thing might come to a screeching halt. "Man, am I ever glad to see you two talking." He turned his attention to Kandi. "Where have you been? I thought that terrorist had finally gotten to you," he said jokingly.

"You are so charming, Clip."

"Thank you, thankuverimuch," Clipper said in his best Elvis voice. "That's why I'm such a hit with the babes."

"Let's talk," Autumn said seriously. "What's the verdict?"

Justin spoke. "I'm going to go ahead and meet with Jarvis and Lester."

"And everybody's OK with this?" Clipper asked, looking at Kandi.

Kandi pulled out her small black Bible and read them the words she underlined at lunch, "'The Lord is laughing at those who plot against the godly, For He knows their judgment is coming.' I decided that if I trusted God I need to really trust him."

"Hmmm," Clipper reasoned. "Redundant but strangely sensible."

"So I'm going through with this whole thing," Justin affirmed, "and that's OK with you, Kandi?"

"You have to, Justin," Kandi said.

"I don't mind coming," Clipper added.

"Me, neither," said Autumn.

"Nope. I was the one who wanted to check out the truck that night, so I'll go alone. I want to do it myself. There's nothing you could do but put yourself in harm's way," Justin replied.

Autumn suggested to the other two, "Why don't we just stick around here and pray?"

"That'd be great if you could," Justin said as he realized the seriousness of the meeting. It wasn't going to be a let's-all-make-it-right experience filled with warm fuzzies and group hugs. He knew this meeting would be filled with glares, threats, innuendoes, and cover-ups. These were the things that made movies watchable, but they certainly didn't make real life livable.

"We can meet out at the practice field," Clipper said.

Justin said, "This could be really weird. After he threatened Kandi, I ran Lester down."

"You did what?" Clipper said in shock.

"I talked to him about this whole thing," Justin replied.

"What did you say?"

"I told him to stay away from Kandi. I said that I was with Kandi and I also saw him and Leafblad. I asked him if they stole the stuff, and he just said no," Justin recounted.

"Did he threaten you or give some explanation about what they were doing?" Autumn asked with a puzzled look on her face.

"Nope. He just sorta looked at the ground and said I couldn't prove anything, and that we'd find out what they were doing sooner or later. I mean, he had me believing for a moment that he really didn't do anything. He put on these sad, puppy-dog eyes like I was persecuting him. I asked him if he or Leafblad let Jarvis know they were there, and he didn't answer me. Just said he had to go."

"Oh, man, you got him," Clipper said, smiling confidently. "Don't you see? You caught him off guard."

"He's scared," Autumn agreed.

"You bet he's scared," Clipper added.

Kandi said nothing.

"My guess is that he'll melt in the meeting and spill the beans, rat on Leafblad to save his own skin, and this whole thing will be over this afternoon," Clipper said.

Kandi finally joined in with a question. "You really think so?"

"Oh, yeah."

"I don't know, Justin. Don't count on it," Autumn said skeptically. "This might get worse before it gets better."

The friends braced themselves for the oncoming collision of beliefs and perspectives. The decision was made: Justin would go it alone. In some ways, it exhilarated Justin to stand up and experience dangerous truth.

Justin spaced out during his last class. It was public speaking and oral interpretation and he had given his speech last Friday. Now other students were scheduled to give theirs. He felt relieved that he really didn't have to think. He could just look intently into the faces of the speakers, nod once or twice a minute, laugh when others laughed, and retreat into his own thoughts about the confrontation that loomed before him.

Every now and then he looked at his fellow students, their laughter, their disposition, their carefree appearance, and he just wanted to run away. *Why am I stuck with this deal? I didn't do anything! If I'm totally clean, why even bother?* He knew the answers to these questions, but he also knew that this issue overshadowed his own well-being. He had to speak out.

As the nervous speakers continued their speeches, Justin took his pencil and wrote down worst case scenarios. Since he had a great imagination, worst case scenarios came a dime a dozen and several dozens to be sure. When he made his mind explore the horrors of his fate, he could just about talk himself into crawling into a hole on any given day. And this wasn't just any given day. These enemies weren't mental or intangible. They walked around on two feet and carried other people's destiny around like old luggage. Justin wrote down a few possibilities:

Leafblad could come down hard on Kandi.

Lester could harass Kandi right out of the state.

Kandi, Autumn, Justin, and Clipper could be accused of the theft.

Justin's heart started pounding. He couldn't write fast enough to list the possibilities. He wadded up the paper, but his brain wouldn't stop the exercise, and his pessimistic mind ran on autopilot.

Lester could sabotage our lives in general.

I could lose my relationship with Kandi.

The possibility of that haunted him because he felt he almost lost her that very day in the tumult of conflict and Lester's threats.

We could be caught up in the middle of a real public mess and have our reputation tainted as suspects and troublemakers.

Kandi's mom barely even knows me. She could write me off in a second for putting Kandi at risk.

This could affect the camaraderie on the basketball team for next season. Lester might be on the team.

The class plodded along with the speed of a chronically arthritic turtle. Justin was exhausted. The last person Justin wanted to be right now was himself. He almost hated himself by the end of the class and wished he could say, "Can we just rewind about four days and start over?" But of course he knew he couldn't. Things had happened.

As the bell rang and students scurried through the daily routine of stolen kisses and rowdy farewells, Kandi eyed Justin down the hall. As if he could feel it through the rude bustling student body that there were two eyes directed at him, he turned around and stared at Kandi. He didn't wave or smile, just stared.

They both felt the intensity of the coming confrontation. Kandi didn't wave or give some phony thumbs-up pose. Justin didn't point at her and wink like the hero of an over-budgeted action thriller. They just stared through waves of students, and a cacophony of echoing voices, knowing that they were both vulnerable, they were both scared, and they were both committed to the truth—no matter what.

By the time Justin walked in through the office door, Lester was sitting in the chair next to Ms. Jarvis' administrative assistant's desk. Lester didn't even look at Justin. He sat there quietly reading a Charles Dickens novel, which really irritated Justin. *"Mr. Cliff Notes" is actually reading a book,* he thought, knowing that Lester presented himself well as a model student. In reality, Lester prided himself on his disdain for books and homework. The outer office was completely vacant, leaving Justin and Lester to make the most of their time before the meeting.

"I thought you were a little smarter than this," Lester said, as he closed his book without marking his spot.

Justin didn't say anything, just looked at the clock and adjusted his watch appropriately.

"You are one sweet chick," Lester mocked.

Justin felt his anger rise. *Don't even say it,* he told himself as his mind selected a choice string of words that he recently discarded from his life before Christ.

"I've always wondered. Are you gay?" Lester hissed quietly. "Is this deal with little Kandi a cover-up for the real Justin?"

No response from Justin. *Forgive us our trespasses as we forgive those who trespass against us.* The phrase came to his mind from nowhere.

Then he remembered Autumn, Kandi, and Clipper were on the grass near the stands of the practice field praying for him. God was in control.

Justin and Lester were finally called into the inner sanctum of the principal's office. Justin couldn't help noticing the irony of the situation. He had spent his entire school career trying to avoid getting into a room like this. Now he forced himself through the door with a shield of values he had adopted as a Christian. Lester slouched in with his arms crossed and a self-righteous scowl on his face. He played the part of victim well as he tapped his index finger on the book and glared at Justin.

Ms. Jarvis was on the phone and gave her visitors a half-hearted wave. She cloaked her responses on the phone with curt yes and no answers. It seemed to Justin that Ms. Jarvis' conversation was a way for her to show her power to the two juniors.

"Great to hear from you, Stella!" she said, obviously trying to end the conversation.

Are they real? Justin pondered the length of the woman's eyelashes. It was a brief diversion to avoid the serious nature of the visit.

In the east wing, Mr. Leafblad strolled casually down the desolate hall. He nonchalantly scanned the locker numbers, then stopped in front of one of them.

He pulled latex gloves out of his sport coat and quickly put them on. From another pocket, he pulled out a small piece of paper. He studied it, looked up and down the hall, then dialed a combination. He lifted the handle and beamed. Mission accomplished.

He took quick inventory of the locker's contents, then paused once again to look up and down the hall. He pilfered through another notebook and came across a neatly typed and stapled paper. He scanned it and casually tucked it back into its place. Reaching into his sport coat, Leafblad pulled out a small paper bag and a roll of duct tape. He taped the paper bag to the top of the locker, which hid the bag perfectly behind an overhanging piece of metal. *She'll never notice,* he thought, admiring his work.

He jerked as he heard the sound of a squeaky wheel on a rolling garbage can and a familiar voice.

"Shoooowee! It's a gettin' mighty late, ma frien'," Felix said from just down other side of the hall. "Whatchu doin' dere, Mr. Leafblad? You mostly be gone by now."

"Oh, hey there, Felix," Leafblad said dryly as his mind raced. He quickly peeled the gloves off his hands and stuffed them in his back pocket. His eyes quickly scanned the locker. *No trace,* he concluded as he kicked it shut with his foot. The sound of the locker slamming made him flinch. He didn't think he kicked it that hard. *Certainly he's too dumb to think that my head in some student's locker was suspicious,* he thought.

"Well, I say, Mr. Leafblad. Whatchu doin' there?" Felix repeated in a jolly voice.

"Not much," Leafblad replied. "What are you up to?"

"My friend. Whatchu think I am doin'?" Felix laughed. "I ain' running for no president. I don' see you here, Mr. Leafblad, this time o' day. Somethin' special goin' on?"

Leafblad shrugged his shoulders, hoping the less he said, the less he'd seem suspicious.

"I know that locker, yeah," Felix said.

"You do?"

"Why, I sho' do. It belongs to a frien' of mine. Number three-six-three."

"Who's that?" Leafblad said, becoming a little more than uptight.

"That's Miss Kandi's locker," Felix said smiling.

"What are you saying?" Leafblad asked. He swallowed back his impulse to lash out at the fool in front of him.

"I just sayin' that's her locker," Felix answered with an innocent smile, just six feet away now. "Are you plannin' some surprise there now, sir?"

Leafblad looked down and saw that one of the plastic gloves had fallen on the floor. Panic rose in his chest.

"You know them kids. They threw a surpise party fo' me yesterday. They is my best friends, dat's why I know. That's her locker. Third one down on the right. So I suspect you jes' goin' to surprise Miss Kandi with somethin'." They were both silent as they stared at each other.

"What do you think, Felix?" Leafblad asked sternly, panic beginning to cloud his thinking. He cracked his knuckles and glared at Felix.

Felix chuckled uncomfortably. "I don' know, Mr. Leafblad. Ah just thought . . . well, ah don't know. Jus saw you putting sometin' dere in her locker an—"

"Felix, you'd better keep your slimy nose outta this. You hear me?!" Leafblad clenched and unclenched his fists. The panic had taken complete control now.

"Oh, Mr. Leafblad, I ain't meant no harm by dat. I was—"

"You just forget what you saw. Do you hear me?"

"Yes, sir."

Leafblad grabbed Felix's arm tightly and said, "That's *really* important. It is none of your freakin' business what I'm doing at this locker. And if you get in my way, you'll be real sorry." Leafblad's voice lowered and grew more threatening. "You love your mom and dad don't you?"

"Ah sho' do," Felix said with a bewildered look on his face.

"I bet you do," Leafblad croaked. "I can make life miserable for you and them. You always said you wanted to take care of them in their old age like they took care of you. Right, re-tard?"

"Yes, sir."

"Then now's your chance. If I so much as hear you've breathed a word about what you saw here, I'll burn their home, and I'll rip the lungs right outta your throat. Got that?"

"Yes, sir," Felix said as his chin quivered. "Ah tol' you. Ah ain't seen nothin."

"Good boy. Just remember I don't threaten people without being willing to follow through. If you value your parents' lives, you'll stay out of this whole mess. *Not a word!*"

Ms. Jarvis lowered her bifocals. "All right, Justin, Lester. How are things?" Neither responded, so she looked a little puzzled. "I believe Justin asked to meet with us, Lester. So here we are."

Justin began tentatively. "Thanks. I don't think this will take long. I don't believe in tattling, and I didn't want to be accused of that. That's why I asked Lester to meet with us." He took a deep breath trying to hide his nervousness.

"Go on," Ms. Jarvis said impatiently.

"This is going to sound like I'm accusing Lester of some-thing, but I just, well like everybody, want to know what hap-pened over the weekend. And I think I have a piece, maybe just a piece of the puzzle. Maybe Lester has a better idea. That's why I asked him to come."

Ms. Jarvis looked at her watch again, expecting to hear another slice of juicy gossip from the student grapevine.

"So it's about the computers?" she asked.

"Right," Justin replied.

Lester stared at the ceiling and let out a big breath of air.

Justin continued. "I work Friday nights, and on the way home I saw Lester's pickup just outside the door next to the computer lab."

Ms. Jarvis' eyes shot over to Lester.

"So you're saying that I did the job," Lester interrupted.

"I'm just saying what I saw, Lester," Justin continued. "I saw Leafblad there too." When Ms. Jarvis didn't respond, Justin went on. "They were loading boxes."

Ms. Jarvis pointed at Justin. "Are you saying that all the way from the road you saw Lester and Leafblad—"

"I pulled into—"

"I?" Lester countered.

"I mean, we."

"Who's we?" Ms. Jarvis asked.

"Myself and three friends, Kandi, Autumn, and Clipper. They work with me."

Ms. Jarvis held up her hand as she wrote notes. "I need to talk to them too. You should know that, Justin."

"Ms. Jarvis, pardon me, but I don't think that's necessary."

Lester interrupted again. "Mr. Leafblad and I were there moving some of his personal stuff out of his room for the summer break. Get this . . . Justin wants you to believe that Mr. Leafblad, Mr. Teacher of the Year, and I broke into the building, spray painted the place, destroyed some of his personal property, and stole computers that Mr. Leafblad worked all year to raise funds for. This is stupid."

Lester turned to look fully at Justin. "Where were you?" Lester asked loudly. "How do we know that you didn't do the job? You were in the parking lot with your friends, and I saw

you. The moment I saw you, you bolted out of there like you'd been caught doing something."

"That's a lie," Justin calmly replied. "We didn't bolt out. Why would I call a meeting with a principal if I did it?"

"You wanted to blame us so that you'd go clean. I saw you there!" Lester said pointing at Justin.

Justin couldn't believe Lester's audacity.

Ms. Jarvis broke in. "Stop this, both of you. Justin, first of all, this is not the way to handle this. If this is your idea of getting to the bottom of this, you are sadly mistaken."

Justin stopped and sat back in his seat.

"I'm not totally in the dark on the events of Friday night involving Lester and Mr. Leafblad. I received an E-mail from Mr. Leafblad today, and he told me about his Friday night work. He even itemized the things he took home. Justin, I can't believe you'd be so arrogant as to grandstand like this."

"Grandstand? I just wanted to tell you what I saw!" Justin said, louder than he should have.

"Don't raise your voice at me!" Ms. Jarvis forcefully commanded.

"I'm sorry. I apologize," Justin said.

Ms. Jarvis stood up from her leather chair. "Apology accepted. Justin, I don't think you had anything to do with the burglary. Lester, I certainly don't have any reason whatsoever to suspect that you and Mr. Leafblad were involved either. I think it's a whole lot simpler than that. Did either of you think that maybe it had something to do with Western High? Now it's time for me to do the talking. I don't want you to breathe another word about this to anyone," Ms. Jarvis said. "We're

going to handle this. Justin, stop watching those reruns of *Murder, She Wrote*, and stay out of my work."

"I'm sorry," Justin said, although he wondered why he felt the need to say so. He just felt relieved, knowing he had done what he felt he should have done and that it all could end. He would gladly back off and let Jarvis handle it. He worried about Lester's attack, but he expected no less. To Justin, this ugly chapter of his life was closed. Now that the meeting was over, he really didn't care who pulled the burglary off. He was just glad Ms. Jarvis had demanded that he stay clear of the investigation.

As Justin went out to his car, he saw Lester peel noisily out of the parking lot, his tires squealing. He figured Lester felt he had been challenged and won. Ms. Jarvis couldn't conceive of Leafblad being involved in something like a burglary which made him Lester's greatest alibi. As Justin shut his car door, he heard a knock on the rear window. He looked through the rear view mirror and saw Clipper, Autumn, and Kandi. Justin had been so consumed in thought he didn't see them returning from the practice field where they had been praying.

Justin opened his door again, got out of the car, and leaned against it. "Hey, guys."

"That didn't take very long," Autumn said.

Kandi tucked in beside Justin, and he put his arm around her shoulders.

"I think it's over," Justin announced with a heavy sigh of relief.

"Over! That's great!" Clipper said with more than a little animation. "That is so cool! What's going to happen next? I bet a press conference. This is so wild! The town is gonna freak when they find out that a teacher pulled it off."

"Whoa! Hold on. I didn't say she's throwing the book at them. I just said we're done with this thing. I did what I had to do, and Ms. Jarvis listened. She said she knew they were there, and she believed they didn't do it—just spring cleaning as far as she's concerned."

The three friends looked at Justin like he had just told a joke with no punch line. They were all sure Lester and Leafblad had something to do with the computer heist. Justin had his doubts as well, but he was able to persuade them they had done everything they should have done. No more. No less. And now they could put it all behind them and concentrate on finals.

The sun hid behind the amber clouds of early evening. Inside the school, crouched in a dingy mop closet, Felix wept. His back trembled as he tried to muffle deep and fearful child-like sobs.

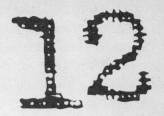

Wednesday morning broke bright and fair. Justin thought about all that was behind him. Yes, it was a great day to be sixteen and living in America. As he drove to school, he cranked up Jars of Clay and rolled down the window. He couldn't wait to see Kandi. It would be great to see her without having this cloud of responsibility hanging over his head. It would be great to goof off, throw away the Lone Ranger mask, and have fun.

As he pulled around into the parking lot, he immediately saw something was different about the scene. All the students were gathered around the front of the main building. He parked his car and noticed that through the mob of students there was a police car and some sort of law enforcement truck.

His heart skipped a beat. He was sure that any moment he would see them taking Leafblad and Lester into custody. *Was Ms. Jarvis simply playing cool when she denied their involvement in the burglary?* he asked himself.

He instinctively ran to the scene. The first officer he saw coming out of the building had a German shepherd on a leash. The officer opened the back of the truck and the dog jumped in.

"This will be a good spot. Can you move back a little? Thanks," a polished female voice said from behind Justin. He turned around and recognized a TV news reporter from a local station. "The mayor is staying true to his word by allocating funds to literally sniff out drugs from the public schools," the reporter began. "At Summit High, many students are protesting their rights to privacy. Mayor Stewart promises that searches like these will be prompted by anonymous tips as well as at random. Will such findings get caught up in a legal battle around the issue of privacy? Only time will tell."

Suddenly three well-known grunge junkies were escorted out of the building. One covered his face and seemed genuinely frightened by what was happening. The other two were cocky and angry looking. They almost seemed proud to be caught up in the scene.

Justin moved closer and heard one officer say to the driver of the squad car, "Just grass." The heavy-set officer shook his head in disgust. "Just a few grams each. They'll be out by the end of the day. But we got the motherload coming. We hit the jackpot if it's what we think it is."

"And what's that?" the other officer asked.

"A mixed bag. It's got to go to the lab, but looks like a methadone . . . ludes . . . and sizable bag of coke. Cantrell's in there questioning her right now," the officer said under his breath.

"A girl, huh?"

"Cute little thing too. Whoda thunk it?"

Then the doors opened again, and what Justin saw made him feel he'd been kicked in the stomach. He saw Kandi, her hands cuffed behind her back, being escorted out of the building by a police officer and a man in a suit. Her eyes were red and hollow. They met his as Kandi and the officers approached the police car. She looked at him without expression. She looked like her emotions had been stripped from her soul in a matter of minutes.

Kandi arrived at school early that morning to talk with her English Lit teacher, and she had a strange encounter with Felix. He was sobbing loudly and clutching his tape player. She tried to talk to him, but he stuffed the recorder in his pocket and ran away.

A few seconds later, everyone was asked to leave the building. Kandi watched the police cars and a swarm of uniformed and plain-clothed policemen enter the building. But hearing her own name over the PA system truly surprised her.

When she arrived in the office, an officer asked her to follow the detective. He led her to her locker where a large dog scratched at it and whined vigorously. The police asked her to open the door. She didn't hesitate, knowing she had nothing to hide.

In a matter of seconds they found the small bag that had been taped to her locker the day before. She stood there in shock. The detectives drilled her with question, after question, after question. Kandi just shook her head and cried. She didn't know how it got there. She didn't know who had supplied it. She had no explanation for anything.

Suddenly a large detective in a blue tweed jacket and thick tie walked up and croaked, "Are you out of your measly minds? Hasn't anybody 'round here ever heard of Mr. Miranda?" He pointed at Kandi. "*This* is the suspect?"

The one uniformed officer nodded. "Course it is."

"You have the right to remain silent. If you give up . . . " The detective's voice echoed through her head, but she only half listened. It was hard to listen when her entire world had fallen into a million pieces. She felt things she had never felt before.

She felt the hands of an attending female police officer taking inventory of her small frame as if she were a piece of furniture. She felt nonexistent. The officer dumped her purse out on the hall floor, searching for more clues.

Last night she had prayed for protection and peace. *And this is what I get,* she thought. Her faith once again suffered the slings of circumstance, and she heard the voice of disbelief once more. The voice of accusation and skepticism intruded her consciousness saying, *"Where is God now? Where are those promises of security and protection? All that junk about help for the innocent and hiding places?"*

But then, as she felt the cold steel handcuffs click over her delicate wrists and accusing stares and questions from all sides, her mind flashed back to a Bible study she'd hosted at her house. She remembered Shawn's words. "Whenever you're going through persecution—and believe me, you will— every time you stand up for Christ or stand up when the truth isn't popular, remember what Jesus went through. He faced accusation. They mocked him right there in front of his own mother. They called him a liar and a blasphemer, the very Son of God. Keep in mind, he was betrayed and deserted by his closest friends. They shamed him. They took turns punching him. They spit upon him. They plucked the beard from his face. They nailed him to a wooden cross beam, naked and bleeding. We will never experience the shame he did."

She couldn't believe it, but she found something strange stirring in her soul. *This is too weird,* she thought. She prayed silently while the female police officer stuffed her belongings into an oversized plastic bag. Kandi couldn't believe what she was praying.

She wasn't praying for help, for vengeance, or even wisdom. She prayed like the Lord stood next to her in the room, holding her hand. She whispered a simple prayer. A prayer of thanksgiving. She had no idea why.

Justin watched Kandi disappear into the squad car. It didn't take much effort to figure out what had happened. He looked everywhere for Ms. Jarvis, but with no success. When the building finally opened, he rushed past the receptionist straight into the office.

"She didn't do it!" Justin said as he burst into the office.

"What are you talking about?" Ms. Jarvis asked, irritated by his lack of courtesy.

"Kandi."

"Who is Kandi?"

"She's the girl who just got arrested for possession. I know her. She's totally clean. She's never touched anything!" Justin said.

"Well, she's in quite a bit of trouble. She had a lot of stuff in her locker. This isn't helping your case, Justin."

"My case?" Justin shot back.

"The fact that you hang around with that girl doesn't help your story that you just happened to be in the parking lot Friday night," Jarvis explained.

"This doesn't make any sense."

"It made perfect sense to me when Leafblad told me his theory. Those drugs cost a lot of money. Where'd she get it? If I were you, I'd stay out of my office until I call you, unless you come in to tell me the truth."

Flabbergasted, Justin couldn't believe what Ms. Jarvis said. He saw his future, his friends, and his reputation being shoved right out of Summit's front door.

He left the office and went straight to his locker, wondering why they picked on Kandi. He wondered, too, if there would be any surprises for him when he opened his locker. As he negotiated his way through the crowded hallway, he ran into Felix. As soon as Felix saw Justin, the older man looked away.

Justin was confused. Felix never acted that way. He never made a habit of ignoring people. Even his walk appeared to be that of a defeated man. He must have found out about Kandi's situation, Justin thought. Maybe he knew a few details that Justin didn't. Justin grabbed Felix's arm, but the custodian jerked away without a single glance.

"What's wrong, Felix. Did you see Kandi?"

"I don't know nothin'."

"They arrested her this morning for drug possession."

Felix just stared at the floor, never looking up to meet Justin's eye. "Didn't you hear what I just said, Felix? Kandi's in trouble."

"I can't help you no ways," Felix said, still looking away.

"What? What in the world are you saying, Felix? You'd do anything for her. I know you. I know what your heart is like." As Justin stared at the custodian, his mind raced. "Felix? Are you hiding something? Do you know something?"

"Can't talk, my friend," Felix said as his eyes finally met Justin's. "You knows I love all of you. But you just goin' to have to forget about ol' Felix for now."

"Tell me what you know!" Justin demanded angrily.

"Now, you leave me alone!" Felix walked away.

Justin started to follow him, but Felix became even more determined to escape.

"I said go away!" He shouted loud enough to stop a few passing students in their tracks. They had never heard this quiet man shout before. Felix turned and walked away quickly as the tears came to his eyes again.

The strange encounter stunned Justin. He thought that the past few days had been the greatest days of Felix's life, and yet now walls of defense and fear had come down. Justin wondered whether Felix had second thoughts about his newfound faith. But that seemed inpossible after all that had happened throughout the past four days. Felix is hiding something, Justin concluded.

Off in the shadows, slouched between a row of lockers and a deserted classroom, Lester watched and smiled. The plan was working like a well-oiled piece of machinery.

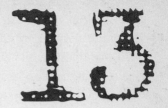

Kandi had never even thought about what a juvenile detention hall might look like. It wasn't a standard lockup full of hardened criminals, but she was definitely not free. Because this was a major arrest, she had to endure the rigors of a strip search. They fingerprinted her, gave her an identification number, photographed her, and allowed her access to the phone for a few minutes.

Her room consisted of a small bed, a toilet, and a sink with cold water. The bed had a mattress cover and a flannel navy blue blanket. Ordinary juvenile offenders weren't treated this harshly, but she was, in their eyes, no ordinary offender. The amount of drugs found in her locker could fulfill the desires of Summit's drug users for at least a couple of weeks. That made her a possible dealer. Dealers were treated as the pond scum of juvenile offenders. Although most suspects are innocent until proven guilty, dealers were treated otherwise.

Kandi leaned on a counter, clutching the phone. "I didn't do anything, Mom. What can I say that'll make you believe me?"

Kandi's mom wept. "I don't know what to believe, Kandi."

"Please, Mom, you've got to believe me. Someone planted the stuff in my locker." Kandi's mom said nothing. "Mom?" The silence grew as tears pooled in the bottom of Kandi's dark brown eyes. Her hands trembled as she realized that even her mother didn't believe her. "What are you thinking?" she tried to say evenly.

"I don't know what to think," her mother said through sobs. "I get a call at work from a police officer who says I need to go to some juvenile detention center, that you've been charged with possession and attempt to distribute ludes and coke. You didn't say anything to me about drugs at the school."

Now, Kandi's anger boiled over. "Because I didn't know, Mom! Do you actually think I'm some drug pusher? I told you! I'd never seen the stuff before they opened my locker. I need you to believe me, Mom. Come get me out of this place," Kandi pled.

"No," Kandi's mom replied.

"What?"

"I said no."

"Mom, you can't do this to me! Why are you doing this?"

"Because I believed your dad's excuses for over a decade, and I'm not going to stand around and let you lie to me and make excuses too."

"Mom, haven't you heard what I've been saying? I'm innocent, with a capital *I*," Kandi exclaimed.

"And I'm angry with a capital *A*."

"Have I ever given you any reason to believe that—"

"I don't want to talk about it. I just want you to be honest with me. If you start telling me how that stuff ended up in your locker, I'll see about getting you out. Think about being honest with me. Will you?"

Kandi pled with exasperation. "Mom, I keep telling you the truth," she moaned through tears, "but it doesn't help. You won't listen to me or believe me. Somebody's out to get me here." Her voice grew louder with her frustration. "I need you to believe me. Ask Justin. Ask Clipper. Those are my friends. They're clean. They've never been in trouble. You like Justin, don't you?" No response from the other end. "Then talk to him. He's gonna call you. I know he will."

The social worker pointed at her watch impatiently, and Kandi concluded, "Mom, I've got to go."

"I'll see you tomorrow."

"What? What about tonight?" Kandi asked.

"I told you. I can't pull you out of there tonight," Kandi's mom said sternly. "Don't ask me to do that. I need you to spend the night there and think about what's going on. I love you, but I'm not prepared to live with these kinds of things. That's why we left your dad."

Kandi couldn't speak. She just shook her head in disbelief and cried. She handed the phone over to the social worker without saying good-bye. The social worker handed her a tissue and escorted her out of the room.

Their shoes hit the concrete floor in the hall echoing through the wing. The social worker handed Kandi off to a large female officer, who twirled her keys around on her index finger. "Sounds like a world of trouble to me," the guard said.

"They said you are mouthing off about getting framed. That's the problem with this generation. You watch movies 'bout people getting off cuz they were framed or because of some wild-eyed conspiracy. It's not that easy, you know. Ain't nobody ever claimed to be responsible for their own actions, their own evil. That's what kills me about workin' here. Everybody's innocent. Or so they say."

When Kandi returned to her holding cell, she crawled onto her bed and laid face down, burying her head in the pillow. She would be arraigned in the morning. She had been told that she would go to the county courthouse, where she would be given an opportunity to plead guilty or not guilty. She felt very nervous about that because she heard she had to fall into a line with adult detainees, just as if she were another criminal. The whole scene overwhelmed her. She had gone to school just like any other day and within moments she entered the world of handcuffs, attorneys, detention guards, and an infinite number of lies and rumors.

With all her tears spent, Kandi escaped to the protectiveness of sleep. Surprisingly she experienced a deep sleep filled with peaceful images, like a small gift from God. As she slept, she dreamed of being a little girl in Amarillo, Texas. Instead of conflict and strife, she enjoyed a harmonious life. Through the misty wonder of the dream she saw a sober father and a happy mother, holding her hand and praying with her before bed. She saw her father smile and sing a love song to her. They turned the light off in her little room, leaving only the gentle radiance

of a night light. She saw them embrace in the doorway, looking at each other for the longest time.

But she was jarred awake by shouts and antagonistic mum-
blings. *Oh,* she thought, *if only I could return to that dream.*

As Kandi sat up from her bed, still in her school clothes,
but devoid of her belt and shoestrings which had been taken
for security reasons, she heard a familiar voice. It was Justin's
voice, pleading his case to the guard. "I really want to see her."

"I'm sorry. I can't let you talk to her until she's been
arraigned." The guard replied.

"Says who?"

"Says me! And that's all that counts."

"That's not fair," Justin said loudly.

"Sorry. How do I know she's not dealing with you and
she's gonna . . . gonna tell you where the rest of the stash is?"

"Do I look like a drug lord to you?"

Kandi could hear the guard's irritation. "Don't you get smart
with me, or you'll be real sorry. I'll throw you out on your ear,"
the guard said.

"I'm not leaving until I see Kandi," Justin said. Kandi
had never heard Justin that angry before. Then she heard
another familiar voice. "Hey, Justin. I heard what happened.
Kandi's here?"

"And who are you?" the guard said defensively.

"I'm Kandi's minister, Shawn Wilkens."

"You don't look like no minister," the guard said. Shawn
kept his black hair in a pony tail and never wore a tie. The
guard had a reason to be a little skeptical. There weren't too
many youth ministers quite like Shawn Wilkens.

"Well, I am. Here . . . look." He pulled out a business card with a clergy symbol on it.

"OK, OK. You can come in, but not the kid. By the way, you don't smoke grass for religious purposes, do ya?" The guard asked, skeptical of everyone.

"Uh, no. I sure don't."

Justin rolled his eyes, and then remembered, "Here, Shawn," he said pulling a Bible out of his back pocket and a note. "It's for Kandi."

"Wait a second," the guard interrupted. "Lemme see that." She grabbed the Bible and the note. She flipped through the Bible and said, "You oughta be glad I'm in a good mood." She tossed the Bible and the letter back to Shawn. Justin glared at the female guard as she handed Shawn a clipboard. "You sign in and note that you're a . . ." she paused, rolled her eyes, and gestured quotations with her fingers, "minister." Then she let out a chuckle.

Kandi sat in a small paneled booth with one chair, a countertop, an ashtray, and a glass partition where Shawn would appear. The guard handed the Bible to Kandi with Justin's note on top. "I hope you don't roll your smokes with the paper," the guard said sarcastically. Kandi took the Bible and the note, gave them a brief glance and waited for Shawn.

Shawn tried to reassure her. "Don't worry about your mom. She's coming around. I think she just needed to hear it from somebody else, and since you called, she's heard it from Justin, Clipper, Autumn, and me. Justin's not taking this very well," he added. "He's really blaming himself for this whole thing." He prayed with her and as he left he said, "Justin's still out in the parking lot. He's been there for about three hours. Do you want me to tell him anything, give him a note?"

"Sure. Could you slide me a pen and paper?"

Shawn shrugged as he pulled out his wallet for a business card. "It's all I have."

"That's fine," Kandi said as Shawn slid his pen and business card under the glass. Kandi wrote a few words on the back and handed the card and pen back to him under the watchful eye of the guard.

After a minute or two the guard once again appeared to take her back to the cell. "I kinda feel like I'm keepin' a celebrity. Got twenty-five calls for you in three hours. Either you really are a pusher, or you got a lotta people that care for you."

Kandi smiled her first smile in a long while. "I think you know the answer to that question."

When Shawn walked out of the building, Justin bombarded him with questions. "How is she? What did she say? The letter! Did you remember to give her the letter? Did she read it?"

"Whoa," Shawn replied. "Yes, I gave her the letter. She's fine. And I'm late for a planning meeting. I can't talk right now," he said as he opened his car door.

"So, you're just gonna leave?" Justin said, shocked by Shawn's casual attitude about the situation.

Shawn put his hand on Justin's shoulder. "Justin, just chill. It's bad, but it's not death row. Head home. There's nothing we can do right now." Shawn got into the car, then rolled down the window. He pulled out his business card with Kandi's note on the back and casually handed it to Justin. "Here. She wanted me to give this to you. I'll see you tomorrow. Don't lose hope, Justin." Shawn drove away.

Justin looked at Shawn's business card:

Shawn Wilkens
Youth Minister
Grove Community Church
555-6971

Justin didn't get it. *Why would Kandi want me to have Shawn's card,* he thought. He stuffed it in his wallet and went back to his car.

The guard locked Kandi's door and walked away, whistling and tossing the keys about two feet in the air. Kandi laid down on the stiff iron bed and pulled Justin's letter from the New Testament he had given her. She wanted to see him, but this was all she had. She read the letter, slowly savoring each word like fine food.

Dear Kandi,

I knew they might not let me see you, so I wrote you this letter. What can I say that would tell you how sorry I am about this whole mess? I left school after homeroom. I said I was sick and I am. It would have been senseless for me to try to make it through the day. When I saw them taking you away in cuffs, I got sick. Really sick. I realized how right you were about Lester's threats. I just want you to know that I'll spend the rest of my life getting you out of this mess if I have to. I know that sounds melodramatic, but it's the truth. I would.

I guess what I want to say is that ever since we first met I've felt a bond with you, and I don't want to see it come to an end. I don't see how you could still care for me, even as a friend, after all you've been through. I've always wanted to protect you, and now here I am and there you are. At this moment, I can't do anything, but if it takes a lifetime, I'll make things right.

I'm not leaving the parking lot. I know it seems kind of weird for me to do this, but if you're stuck in there all alone, the least I can do is be close by and pray. Can you believe Dad's letting me? He's almost as mad as I am about the whole thing. He thinks a whole lot of you.

We're all praying for you. I haven't stopped praying since this morning—puking and praying. Not exactly manly, but it's the truth, and I know how much you value the truth. So there it is. I'm a spiritual warrior, who's highly hacked off and a little bit queasy. I just keep telling myself that God's in control. Do you believe that? He is, Kandi. And somehow, some way he'll bring everything into the light of truth. Like Shawn says, "It's hard to keep truth under

wraps. It keeps wiggling its way out of the bag." The
truth is squirming, Kandi. And all we have to do is
wait for it. It'll happen.

Love,
Justin

P.S. We're meeting tomorrow afternoon about the
whole thing. A big one. Leafblad, Lester, Clipper, Clip-
per's parents, my Dad, Mrs. Jarvis, and who knows
who else. I might get the chance I've prayed for—a
chance to clear this whole thing up.

Kandi smiled and put the letter to her lips. She then picked
up the Bible and read, in awe of how God led her to Scriptures
that were so personal:

"O God my Rock," I cry, "why have you forsaken me?
Why must I suffer these attacks from my enemies?"
Their taunts pierce me like a fatal wound;
again and again they scoff, "Where is that God of yours?"
But O my soul don't be discouraged. Don't be upset.
Expect God to act!
Psalm 42:9–11

Kandi smiled in the darkness as she closed her eyes that
night in a strange and frightening place. *I'll trust you with this,*
God. You carried the cross for me, Lord. I can trust you with my
life, wherever you lead me. Even if it's into a place like this. My
heart's in your hand. I'll trust you.

It was almost midnight when someone knocked on Clipper's door. His dad had awoken and heard his soft sobs. "Clipper? Can I come in?" his dad called through the door. "Are you all right?"

"I'm OK," Clipper said faintly.

Mr. Hayes came into the dark room and turned on the lamp. He sat on the bed and Clipper sat up. "It's like nobody believes what we saw, Dad. Kandi's mom wouldn't even go get her tonight. Ms. Jarvis thinks we're involved in a drug thing; half the school is looking at us like we're underworld scum. It's like they've forgotten who we are."

Mr. Hayes put his hand on his son's shoulder. "I'm upset too. But you've got to believe me. This thing is going to be straightened out."

Clipper rubbed his face with his palms, sniffed, and cleared his throat. "Another thing that hurts so bad is that Felix is avoiding us like the plague. I walked right up to him, and he wouldn't even look me in the eyes. I think somebody's told him that he shouldn't hang around with us or something. Saturday night he accepts Christ, and it's the best thing that has ever happened to him. For all his life people have made fun of him and treated him like some kind of lowlife bother. We treat him like one of us and then he writes us off."

His dad just sat and listened intently.

Clipper continued, "You believe us, don't you?"

"Course I do."

"But that doesn't seem to matter now, does it?"

"Maybe not. But Clipper, think about it. The people you are talking about—outside of Felix, what's the common denominator?"

"Common denominator?"

"What's different about them? What separates them from us?"

Clipper looked at his dad strangely and shrugged his shoulders.

Mr. Hayes answered his own question. "They don't have the same Father. They aren't committed to the same God that we are. They don't believe us because they are running on a different set of rules. You've grown up with Lester. You know he's looking out for himself and not the truth. Ms. Jarvis is a fine lady, but she doesn't know you like I know you. I'd be surprised if she'd know your name if you passed her in the hall. That's not your fault. I've made a commitment to stand up for you, and I believe in you and Justin. I'm scared too. It's a mess. God said we'd have troubles, right? But He's the overcomer and He's made us overcomers too."

Clipper nodded, still anxious.

"Let's get some sleep. I'll see you in the morning, and I'll be there for the meeting after school. We'll face the music and fight this one together."

"OK."

Mr. Hayes left, and Clipper turned the lamp off, peacefully drifting off to sleep.

Justin woke up fifteen minutes before his alarm clock went off. It surprised him a little. That usually only happened on game day. This was the day of the big meeting and adrenaline flooded his veins. He showered and dressed. He usually spent very little time getting ready, just picking out the first shirt that fell out of the drawer and his freshest smelling jeans. But this morning, he scanned his wardrobe like an attorney ready to argue a case before the supreme court.

"Khaki pants? No, too stuffy. Wear jeans. Don't be a dork. OK, jeans. Blue or black? Go with the black. Nope, don't wanna look like the bad guy. But black isn't always bad; it's formally informal. What does that mean? Have I gone crazy? Wear the true blues or faded? Faded."

After the pants, he repeated the same scenario with his shirts. After the whole dressing fiasco, he laughed at himself and thought, *This must be what girls go through every morning!*

When he finished, he looked in the mirror long and hard. Full front. Profile. He went through a mental checklist. Teeth brushed. Deodorized. He tossed that in his duffel bag. He might need it later. He thought he might have overdone it when he walked into the kitchen and his three-year-old brother called out to him, "Justin! It ain't Sunday."

Oh brother, Justin aptly thought.

His dad walked in, looping his tie around the knot as he scooted around the table to the cupboard. "Hey, guys. Lookin' sharp, Justin."

Justin rolled his eyes. "Thanks for noticing. Do you need me to drop Christopher off at the preschool?"

"That'd be great. Ellen's running a little late," his dad replied. Ellen was Christopher's mom and his stepmom. She and Justin's dad had been married for almost six years after Justin's mom walked out of their house and out of their lives. Today was nerve-racking, but nothing like what he remembered about those days.

Justin's dad called out, "Ellen, have you seen the Raisin Bran?"

A muffled voice replied, "No, honey. I think we're out."

"Guess I'll have to eat the 'Co-co Cablams,'" he said, smiling and shrugging his shoulders. He tried to hide the fact that he liked kid's cereals. He quickly poured the cereal and chased it into the bowl with an overdose of milk.

Justin took a quick inventory and quickly found the Raisin Bran. He picked out the box and shook it. "Here's the bran, Dad." His dad looked up just as he took a bite and said in false disappointment. "Oh darn . . . And I've already poured the milk."

"You think your intestines can do without the fiber, old man?" Justin said jokingly.

"Watch it."

"Pretty soon you're gonna be drinking those canned old folks' shakes."

"You're treading on thin ice, boy."

"I'll see you after school in the office?"

"Wouldn't miss it," his dad replied as Justin headed for the garage door. "Justin?"

Justin turned around. "Yeah?"

"I'll be praying for you."

"Thanks."

"Keep your cool."

"Cucumber cool, Dad," Justin said with a smile. "Come on, Christopher."

After Justin dropped Christopher by the preschool, he hurried on to Clipper's house. When he got there, Clipper was waiting outside and he hopped in. They made their way through the suburban maze of morning traffic to Summit High School.

"So, how long did you stay out there last night," Clipper asked.

"About 12:30," Justin said.

"What did your dad say?"

"He didn't say anything."

"I can't believe it," Clipper said. "My dad would hang me by my toenails if I stayed out that late."

"So would mine. But he knew I wasn't going anywhere," Justin said.

"What did you do out there?" Clipper asked.

"Prayed mostly," Justin replied as he flipped the shade on the windshield to block the morning sun.

"And what else?"

"Worried a lot too. I hope the worrying doesn't cancel out the praying," Justin said with a smile.

Clipper downed the last few swallows of chocolate milk from the plastic half-gallon jug he had swiped from the fridge. He wiped the brown mustache from his face and asked, "You ever wonder how we got in this whole mess?"

"They say curiosity killed the cat," Justin said, feeling very small and guilty.

"Is Autumn going to be at the meeting this afternoon?" Clipper asked after a short pause.

"Not if I have anything to do with it," Justin replied.

"Why?"

"Every time they wanted to get to me, they went for Kandi. Now they got Kandi. Got her real good. It's like they know, if we want to get to Justin, get a friend, or better yet a girl. I don't want anybody else, especially a girl taking the heat for me," Justin said and then shook his head in disgust. "That's low, ya know. Really low. I don't think I could live with myself if Autumn took a hit for this whole thing."

"If I were them, I'd stay away from her," Clipper said. "She asked me for a ride one time. It was for that pep rally right before the tournament started. I picked her up. I was kind of wondering what her dad was like. I remembered he's just a preacher. No sweat. Then he opened the door. Whoa! He looked to be about six-foot-seven, really big. No kidding, he had that deep Darth Vader/CNN type voice."

"I know. I called the other day to talk to her, and he answered. For a moment I thought it was the voice of God himself," Justin agreed.

"It's better in person."

"No way!" Justin exclaimed.

"Way."

Justin wheeled the old Caprice into the student parking lot. As they moved to find a parking space, they noticed the stares they were getting from everyone. Clipper said under his breath, "Either we're really strange looking today or we're carrying the Ebola virus."

"This whole thing stinks," Justin said gritting his teeth. "Who do they think we are?"

"The way I see it, we're either narks or drugees. Can't win for losing. Friends of that infamous drug queen, Kandi," Clipper said.

"Pretty wild reputation, my boy," Justin said smiling.

Melissa, a casual friend of Kandi's and a member of their youth group, cornered Justin in the hall just before first period. She blasted him with questions. "Where've you been? I tried calling you all last night? What's going on with Kandi? Did she really do it? Was she selling heroin?"

"Would you cool it, Melissa?" Justin said angrily. "I can't believe you! If you don't know the answer to those questions, you are way out of touch. Can we take this one question at a time?" Justin took a deep breath, then continued. "I went to the detention center, and I didn't get back until after midnight. Kandi's there, as you already know. And no, she's not selling heroin to raise money for her college fund."

"Whew, that's a relief," Melissa said.

Justin couldn't believe she took his sarcastic response seriously.

During first period, what Justin had dreaded most happened. A student messenger walked in and handed the teacher a note. She read it, then looked at the class. "Justin, got a note here for you." She gave him a forced half smile. "Don't forget your books."

The last comment about not forgetting his books brought images of firing squads. Obviously, he was going somewhere, and he wouldn't be back for at least an hour. Perhaps to Siberia, Alcatraz, or Patmos. Or maybe a work camp for the criminally insane, where he would be forced to clean floors with a toothbrush. He visualized beans and rice every day. He imagined his father weeping as authorities threw him into a boiling pit of hot lava, or even worse—having to meet with Ms. Jarvis.

As he walked down the hall to the office, his heart raced and then he came to his senses. *This is crazy! What's she gonna do to me? What can she do to me? What if she expels me? What if she accuses me of being something I'm not? What difference does it make if she wrecks my future and brands me for life as some kind of communist dissident?* After such a heroic thread of thought, such a flash of undaunted courage, he suddenly became woozy again.

He worked himself into a panic of Clipper Hayes proportion. *Lord, settle me down,* he prayed silently. But his heart continued to race. He feared he would be a muttering idiot in her office. A sideshow freak. He could hear the carnival barker, *"Come one! Come all! Feast your eyes on the sheer terror of the Summit High muttering idiot! Once a normal student until he snapped under pressure! You'll cringe at the sight of this sixteen-year-old student who foams at the mouth at the mere mention of computer burglaries."*

But the moment his hand touched the office doors, the visions of panic and humiliation vanished. He cooled down. In Clipper's words—cucumber cool. He smiled at the receptionist, who barely glanced up at him while doodling on her desk calendar. "She's waiting," the receptionist said.

Ms. Personality, Justin thought. He walked in still baffled by his own serenity. *Must be the Lord. It sure ain't me,* he thought. He cleared his throat to announce his arrival into the inner sanctum of administration. "Hi, Ms. Jarvis. You wanted to see me?"

Ms. Jarvis looked up, stood, and gave him her usual stuffy greeting. "Hello, Justin. Have a seat please." They both sat down. "Glad I could pull you out of that class of yours for a few seconds," she said looking down at her Daytimer. She avoided eye contact with him. "Guess you're wondering why I called you in here."

"The question did pass through my mind," Justin said with a nervous chuckle. Ms. Jarvis didn't laugh.

"I wanted to ask you about our meeting. I'd like us to, shall we say, prepare for what will happen." Her tone became even more serious and assertive. "Actually, I thought we might be able to clear some things up and then we might not even need to have a meeting. Make sense?"

"That'd be great but—"

"Because the way I see it," Ms. Jarvis said, interrupting Justin midsentence, "I mean, from my perspective this thing is getting way out of hand. I've already had a number of calls from different people who want to be in this meeting and frankly, I don't . . . I mean, a conspiracy involving Mr. Leafblad? He's been Teacher of the Year four times at Summit. He was a finalist three years ago for the national award. We sent him to Orlando. He made the news. And now he's supposedly involved in a burglary?" She looked down at her fingernails and smiled. "I'm sorry, Justin, it just doesn't match up. I've heard of a double life, but that's absurd."

"Let me just go over some of the reasons—" Justin interjected.

"No. You listen to *me*," Ms. Jarvis said tapping her pointed index finger on the cowhide desk protector. "This is getting crazy, and you are in way over your head. Mr. Leafblad is bringing in a lawyer, and the lawyer's mouth is watering at the prospect of a defamation of character suit. This is serious business, and we, I mean the school, can't afford this kind of publicity, especially when you don't have a leg to stand on. You'd better be prepared to play hardball if you actually want this meeting to happen. A detective from the police department will be here. It could get ugly for you."

Justin felt the blood drain from his face. His stomach felt
queasy. "It doesn't matter, Ms. Jarvis. We didn't start this thing.
Kandi's in jail for—"

"She's being detained—"

"What's the difference? She's locked up for something that
she didn't do."

"You don't know that!" Ms. Jarvis shot back.

"Oh, yes, I do! Kandi's, well—"

"Your girlfriend?"

"Yeah. I guess you can say that.

"Love is blind, Justin. Have you ever heard that saying?"

"A couple times."

"Look. I've called you here to ask you, to beg you. Just
drop the whole thing so I can clear my desk of all these letters
and legal innuendoes and parents' phone calls and faculty
threats. I'm not the enemy here."

Justin jumped in. "I never said that you were."

"I have always enjoyed having you as a student here. I've
never had any problem with you, but just step back and put two
and two together. This Kandi moves into town and all of the
sudden you're in the middle of all of this controversy and—"

"*She's* a victim in this!"

"Look," Ms. Jarvis said, then paused to take a deep breath.
She stood up from her desk and walked over to the window.
Not even looking at Justin, she began her proposal. "I want to
make a deal just between you and me. Maybe you are right.
Maybe Kandi isn't into drugs, and if she is, she'll get caught
sooner or later. I think I can get the charges dropped. In my
opinion, the police made a lot of mistakes. But let's not get into

that. Let's just drop the whole mess. Mr. Leafblad wants this to stop. I talked to him early this morning, and he's hurt by this, but he's willing to forget it, if we can move on. Insurance is paying for our losses. The only thing we gain from this thing, especially if any of this gets into the courts, is a bad image."

Justin's mind raced. Drop the whole thing and Kandi's free. The whole thing would be over. He thought about the tone of the meeting. Justin even speculated that perhaps Ms. Jarvis directed the cover-up. She surely seemed willing to let the insurance pay for the damage and to move on. *Nope,* he thought, *she's not involved. She just wants it to be over.*

"Do you understand?"

Justin answered, "I do."

"Then it's off?"

Justin paused again. *What would Kandi want?* Justin thought about how much he admired her strength. She was most beautiful when she was strong. He wished he could hold her and protect her. But allowing her to endure the humiliation of even a simple slap on the hand for something she did not commit? Would that be justice? Would that be truth in the eyes of God? Would that truly be freedom? He knew the answers to those questions. She wanted innocence, not some minor technicality to buy her freedom. Justin gathered his books that were laying beside him on the floor and stood.

"No. It's not off."

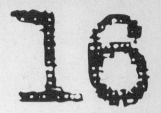

16

Originally the meeting was scheduled to take place in Ms. Jarvis' office, but as the time drew near and the number of attendees grew larger, it was moved to the administrative conference room. Justin sat nervously waiting for his dad. The people who gathered there were as somber as if they were attending a funeral. Mr. Leafblad sat stone-faced, with arms crossed over his belly.

Justin recognized the tall, lean man sitting next to Mr. Leafblad. Billboards all over town bore pictures of the well-dressed man. "Don't get mad. Get Steven! Steven Pickney, attorney-at-law, fighting for what's coming to you."

Justin hated the commercials more than he hated the billboards. It seemed Mr. Steven Pickney cared about wearing expensive Italian suits and being in the limelight more than he cared about the truth. Justin figured Mr. Pickney was salivating over the chance to take on the school board.

Detective Valdez was the exact opposite of Steven Pickney. He was a small Hispanic man who wore a corduroy jacket over a tan dress shirt and a tie that was so wide, it almost seemed like some sort of retro statement. *No way,* Justin thought. *He's just dressing like he probably has for years. He's the only one who came into the room without an attitude.*

Lester sat slouched in a chair until his dad elbowed him to straighten up. He gave Justin a "drop dead" glance, then stared at the door like a caged animal. Lester's dad was intimidating simply by the heavy scowl he wore on his face. He glanced at his watch every few seconds or so, as if he had better things to do with his time. Justin knew this wasn't the first meeting he'd attended on Lester's behalf.

Justin waved with a forced half smile when Clipper and his dad came in for the meeting. Clipper looked both proud and a little embarrassed. *This is like a nightmarish father/son get-together,* Justin thought to himself.

Clipper and his dad, Frank, had never been to a meeting like this before. They had nothing to compare it with, but they felt outmanned, especially when they saw Lester's lawyer with his sleek laptop ready to fire off writs and appeals. Clipper whispered to his dad, "You think we should have called Uncle Clarence?"

Clarence, Clipper's uncle, was a tax attorney. Mr. Hayes looked strangely at his son, half smiling. "Not unless this is an audit."

Justin's dad, Mark, finally arrived. Mark walked over and shook hands with Mr. Hayes. He then introduced himself to Leafblad and Pickney, who both ceremonially shook hands with him. Then he shifted his attention to Lester's dad, who refused Mark's open hand. He sat there glaring at Mark, so Mark simply smiled and sat down.

Detective Valdez leaned forward and spoke in a soft voice to Justin, Clipper, and Lester. "It would help me with my report if I could get a driver's license number from all three of you."

The three boys consented. Lester gave Justin a triumphant smile that implied, *I'm not the only suspect here.* Justin's heart jumped as he reached in his back pocket for his wallet. It reminded him of how serious this whole ordeal had become. As Justin fumbled through his wallet for his driver's license, a business card fell to the floor. He reached to pick it up and noticed handwriting. It looked like Kandi's. *But how did it get in my wallet?*

He turned the card over and realized it was on the back of Shawn's business card that Shawn had given him the night before! *How stupid could I possibly be!*

Justin read the words that Kandi had hoped he'd read the night before: *Find Felix! Listen to his tape player. Might help you! Love, Kandi.*

Justin's mind raced. *I've got to get out of this meeting.*

"Uh, Justin?" Valdez said, "Your license?"

"Oh, right, my license," he said as he pulled his license out and handed it over to Valdez.

"What's up?" Justin's dad whispered to Justin. "You look like you've just seen a ghost."

Justin didn't answer. He just stared at the door, trying to think of a reason to leave the meeting and find Felix. He prayed silently, "God! What should I do? Get me out of here!"

The detective finished copying the information and handed the licenses back to the three young men.

Ms. Jarvis paid no attention to any of them. Justin felt the tension in the room. No one spoke as they waited for the principal to begin. Moments passed, then she finally slid her glasses off her face and placed them in their case. She had just opened her mouth to speak when someone knocked at the door. Detective Valdez opened it and looked up at the huge man filling the doorway.

"And who are you?" Ms. Jarvis said in an exasperated tone.

"I'm Pastor Eli Sanders," he replied in a deep bass voice.

Ms. Jarvis was still at a loss.

"Autumn Sanders' dad," he continued, hoping to solve the riddle for Ms. Jarvis.

"This meeting doesn't have anything to do with Autumn," Ms. Jarvis said, her voice sounding perplexed.

The African-American preacher found the last empty seat and made himself at home. "It most certainly does, Ms. Jarvis. She was with Justin, Kandi, and Clipper that night. I imagine Justin mentioned that to you. Right, son?"

Justin gulped, "Yes, sir."

Ms. Jarvis spoke. "I must have forgotten. But there's really no reason for you to be here because—"

"I'll stay," he said firmly. He placed his big King James Bible on the conference table with a heavy thud. Then he smiled and said, "You know, I have always respected you, Ms. Jarvis. People have said some mighty nice things about your leadership capabilities. All true, all true, I'm sure. I just wanted to see you in action, especially when my daughter and her dear friends' reputations are on the line."

"All right," Ms. Jarvis said nervously, as her eyes shot down to her Daytimer.

Rev. Sanders gave Justin's dad a wink and a knowing smile.

Ms. Jarvis turned the meeting to business. "Let's get straight to work. I promised Mr. Leafblad that he would be able to make a brief statement."

Mr. Leafblad opened a brown notebook where he had scrawled a few notes. His lawyer leaned over and whispered some final instructions. Leafblad cleared his throat and began. "I'm sure all of you must be aware of how stressful the past few days have been on me."

He stopped appearing to be choked up. Mr. Pickney, his attorney, gave him an encouraging pat on the back.

"As you know, I've had a long and distinguished career at this school. I love it here. Sure, I could have gone on to be a professor at Indiana State or some other school, but I love kids. Always have. And the past few days have been my worst nightmare—to see kids I have loved and taught turn their backs on me and even accuse me of stealing school property. I'm depressed. I haven't been myself. What would make them accuse me of this? I've tried to reason this through but to no avail. Do they mean to destroy my record or my career as a public school teacher? This is my life!"

His tone became firmer, less melancholy and more assertive. "And to think that these, these students would want to strip me of all I've worked for. I just can't stand around here and watch them do it." He clenched his fist and shook the notebook in the air. "I'm not going to let them destroy me with their lies. And that's all they are. Blatant lies!"

Mr. Pickney once again put his hand on Leafblad's shoulder, but this time trying to silence him for the moment. Then Pickney stood and addressed the group. "Mr. Leafblad has proven to be an outstanding teacher and loyal public servant. If these absurd accusations do not cease and desist, we will have no other choice than to bring legal action against the school and all parties involved in this malicious attempt to assassinate his character and reputation."

Ms. Jarvis aimed an obvious glare at Justin.

"I helped pay for those computers!" Leafblad yelled out, spewing emotional acid across the room.

Ms. Jarvis pointed her finger at Justin. "Justin? What do you have to say? Keep in mind that there is a lawyer present."

Justin's dad interjected smoothly, "He knows who is here, Ms. Jarvis. Go ahead, Justin."

"I can only say what I know. Friday night Clipper, Kandi, Autumn, and I saw Lester and Mr. Leafblad loading large boxes into Lester's pickup. And then two days later, I hear about a burglary on the news."

The lawyer jumped in. "If that's all you know, then what are we even doing here? Mr. Leafblad was taking home personal belongings. This is absurd! I should slap you with a civil court summons for trying to crucify this man's—"

"Crucify?" Rev. Sanders jumped in, matching the lawyer's volume and then some. "Nobody's getting crucified today, Mr. Pickney. I wholeheartedly object to your adversarial tone. Why don't you let Justin finish?" Rev. Sanders wasn't a lawyer, but for a moment he sounded like a superior court judge. "Go ahead, Justin," Rev. Sanders said as he sat back to listen.

Justin continued. "On Monday, Lester seemed very defensive. He threatened Kandi. He said if she didn't keep quiet about what she saw that he'd make life miserable and ruin her reputation."

"Were you there?" Pickney asked forcefully, sarcastically.

"No, I wasn't," Justin answered.

"Then what you claim Lester said is hearsay!" Pickney shouted.

Everyone looked at one another, wondering if they were in a court or a conference room.

Justin looked over at Ms. Jarvis. She shook her head with her nose in her notes as if she didn't believe a word he was saying. It took every ounce of his restraint he had not to slam his fist on the table and walk out.

"You miss the court, don't you, Mr. Pickney?" Rev. Sanders observed.

"What do you mean by that?" Pickney asked.

"You keep making your objections, defending your client, but this is not a courtroom. It's not even a deposition. This is a school. We're just trying to solve some riddles here. Right, Ms. Jarvis?" She didn't respond. "We want to find out who's telling the truth here. Right, Ms. Jarvis?" He waited this time until she nodded her head in agreement. "The way I was reared, if you had a misunderstanding, and you talked through it thoroughly, the truth would come out. Justin, we're sorry for the interruption. You can continue now."

This caught Justin off guard. He was so enthralled with Rev. Sanders's distinguished manner of negotiation that he lost his place. "Where was I?" he finally mumbled after a second or two.

Frank Hayes came to the rescue. "Justin, I think you were talking about the threats Lester made."

"Allegedly made," Lester's dad added.

"Right. Allegedly made," Frank relented.

Justin continued. "Lester made these threats. I talked with Ms. Jarvis about what I saw, then Kandi ended up in jail."

Lester's dad stood straight up and pointed his thick finger at Justin. "Because she's a druggie! You want to know why she's in jail, because she had drugs in her locker. This isn't Watergate. This isn't a cover-up. She's where she ought to be, where all dope addicts ought to be! She had five ounces of cocaine in her locker."

"A lot more than that, she had ludes!" Leafblad added.

Finally Officer Valdez spoke up. "Funny . . . you're right."

"What are you saying?" Leafblad said, still seething.

"I just said you're absolutely right. There were more than five ounces of coke in the locker, a lot more. Over eleven ounces. The report just came back from the lab today. And it wasn't pure. Good thing she didn't sell it, or she would have had some pretty angry customers. Probably only an ounce of it was the real stuff. The rest was powdered sugar."

He stopped, licked the lead of his pencil, and continued while writing. "No reason for me to talk about that. We're still working on it. I just thought we had more confidentiality with the case. We never released that information to the press."

"That's enough of this nonsense. You're trying to make this man," Pickney said, pointing to Leafblad, "into a criminal. I thought we could solve this thing amicably. My client had no desire to see this scene played out in the newspapers, but it seems we have no choice. You want a fight? You've got it!" He stood, closing his laptop and grabbing his jacket.

Ms. Jarvis stood up and begged, "Please, let's not do this. This meeting isn't over."

"It is as far as I'm concerned, Annette!" Mr. Leafblad erupted, waving off Ms. Jarvis' plea. "I poured my life into this place. I've been here ten years longer than you! Ten years! And now you have the nerve to drag me into this mess. Where is all the loyalty you've been preaching about in faculty meetings? Loyalty? Teamwork? What a disgrace!"

The two men headed toward the door. Detective Valdez stood. "I would strongly advise you to stay. At least for a little while, Mr. Leafblad, and I'd advise counsel to stay also."

Pickney seized the moment. "What in the name of law and order are you inferring, officer? Do you have any witnesses? You actually think there might be some legitimacy to this claim? Do you have any proof?"

"He could have gotten access to the girl's combination. He had a motive," Valdez said while drumming his fingers on the table.

Pickney laughed. "I can't believe I'm even listening to this. He also could have been up in the book depository in Dallas in 1963 when the president was assassinated."

Valdez smiled slyly and spoke softly, "As a matter of fact, he could. Where were you living in '63, Mr. Leafblad?" Most everyone laughed.

The laughing was cut short as Felix stumbled into the conference room with vacuum and a large rubber garbage can. Justin couldn't believe it. He had prayed for a way out of the room so that he could find Felix, never believing the man would walk right through the door.

Felix's eyes widened when he spotted Mr. Leafblad.

Leafblad instinctively yelled at Felix, "Get out, Felix! This is a private meeting!"

Felix studdered, "I ain't done nothing, Mr. Leafblad. I promise."

Justin stood up and moved toward Felix. "I need your tape player, Felix."

"I can't do it, Justin," Felix replied.

Ms. Jarvis was stupified. "For heaven's sake, what is going on? Felix, we're in a meeting."

"Felix, give me the tape recorder," Justin asked again as he stood eye to eye with him. Felix's trembling hand pulled the small recorder out of his front pocket.

"Sit down, Justin!" Ms. Jarvis said assertively.

Justin sat down, but now he had the tape player in his hands. He nervously found the controls and pressed rewind as the group continued to question Leafblad. Justin didn't even know what he was listening for.

Leafblad pointed his finger at Felix. "He's friends with these kids," he said, speaking of Clipper and Justin, "and you wonder why the alarm never went off? He had the keys and the code for the security system. It all makes a lot of sense to me. He's the one you should question."

Justin paid no attention to Leafblad as he continued to listen and rewind feverishly. He trusted Kandi. Something important was on that tape.

"I done kept ma mouth shut," Felix said, pleading.

"Clipper, Justin," Ms. Jarvis asked accusingly, "is Felix involved in this?"

Clipper looked over at Justin, who had a strange smile on his face. "I don't even know what you're saying, Ms. Jarvis," Clipper said innocently. "Did we ever say anything about Felix?"

"It's obvious they were working together," Pickney interjected. "Sort it out yourself, Jarvis." He turned to Mr. Leafblad. "Come on, we've been here long enough."

Rev. Sanders simply stood in front of the door. Pickney and Leafblad had nowhere to go.

Finally Felix exploded. "Dat does it!" he screamed. His whole body shook in fury. "I been thinkin' and thinkin' what I should do."

Leafblad couldn't keep silent. "I think you'd better quit while you're ahead."

"Ain't no quittin', Mr. Leafblad," Felix replied with heart racing and fists clinched.

"I'm going to tell you one more time, Felix," Jarvis warned, pounding her fist on the table for emphasis, "Leave now, or you'll be fired. You are being disrespectful and belligerent."

"Go on then. Go on an' fire ole Felix. But it ain't goin' to do you no good."

Leafblad's face turned crimson with rage.

"He told me he goin' kill my daddy an' mama if I told you that, but I'd like to see the ole boy try."

"Who put this idiot up to this?" Pickney, the lawyer demanded an answer.

Jarvis first went for Justin. "Did you do this?"

Justin held his hands in surrender, and before he could
speak his father jumped in. "I can't believe you, Ms. Jarvis.
How dare you start accusing people like that."

Felix shouted to Jarvis, "They ain't nobody put me up
to this!"

"We'll see you in court!" Pickney said over the chaotic conference room.

"Sit down, Leafblad," Valdez demanded and then turned to
Pickney. "If I were you, I'd earn my wage and give this man
some legal advice," he said gesturing to Leafblad.

"What's there to defend?" Pickney said, shaking a finger in
Felix's face. "This man's a nut case. Next thing you know he's
gonna be saying the computers were being abducted by the
cast of *The X-Files!*"

Huge tears rolled down both sides of Felix's face. "I may
not be as smart as you, but I ain't no crook."

"Let me guess," Pickney said smiling. "This is your star wit-
ness." He shook his head and said under his breath, looking
Felix in the eyes, "I eat these guys for breakfast on the stand.
I'll have his head spinning. And before he knows it, the truth
will come out and the real victim, Mr. Leafblad, will be exonerated with a large sum from the school system. You folks are
pathetic." Pickney zipped his laptop carrying case and headed
for the door. "I said come on, Mr. Leafblad." Leafblad stood up
to follow.

"*I* said sit down, Mr. Leafblad," Valdez said firmly. Leafblad
sat down.

"You still just have his word against my client's word." He
turned to Leafblad. "Did you ever threaten this man's parents?"

Leafblad said with force, "I most certainly did not. That's absurd. I haven't said three words to him all year!"

Justin finally jumped in. "You most certainly did!"

"Do you have any proof?" Leafblad said sarcastically, shaking his head in disgust.

Justin pressed the play button and the stunned group listened to the muffled sounds that Felix had recorded:

"Well, I say, Mr. Leafblad. Whatchu doin' there?"

"Not much. What are you up to?"

"My friend. Whatchu think I am doin'? I ain' running for no president. I don' see you here, Mr. Leafblad, this time o' day. Somethin' special goin' on?"

The clamorous debate grew hush as the tape played. Leafblad stood frozen in shock.

Felix: *I know that locker, yeah.*

Leafblad: *You do?*

Felix: *Why I sho' do. It belongs to a frien' of mine. Number three-six-three.*

Leafblad: *Who's that?*

Felix: *Dat's Miss Kandi's locker.*

All eyes were on Leafblad. Adrenalin pumped through Justin's veins as he, too, listened again to the words he had heard for the first time just seconds before. He instinctively wanted to climb over the table and pin Leafblad to the floor when he heard the threat Leafblad made at Felix.

Leafblad: *That's* really *important. This is none of your freakin' business what I'm doing at this locker. And if you get in my way you'll be real sorry. You love your mom and dad, don't you?*

Felix: *Ah sho' do.*

Leafblad: *I bet you do. I can make life miserable for you and them. You always said you wanted to take care of them in their old age like they took care of you. Right re-tard?*

Felix: *Yessir.*

Leafblad: *Then now's your chance. If I so much as hear you've breathed a word about what you saw here, I'll burn their home, and I'll rip the lungs right outta your throat. Got that?*

Leafblad shouted, "Give me that!" He lunged for the recorder, but Rev. Sanders sat him back down with one hand on Leafblad's shoulder. And the room became quiet again as he continued.

Leafblad: *Good boy. Just remember I don't threaten people without bein' willing to follow through. If you value your parents' lives, you stay out of this whole mess. NOT A WORD!*

Justin stopped the recorder. The blood drained from Leafblad's face. He gripped the side of the table, looking weak and frail.

"I believe my daughter bought you some quality merchandise, Felix," Rev. Sanders said smiling.

Valdez walked over to where Leafblad was seated and put his hand on his shoulder. "Do you have any explanation for that?" he asked sternly.

Pickney immediately answered, "Mr. Leafblad chooses not to comment at this time."

Leafblad started to speak, but Pickney said loudly, "NO COMMENT!" Leafblad rubbed his nose and then folding his hands on the table, he said, "No comment."

"I suppose you'll want to speak with us further on this matter," Pickney said while pulling out a card from his suit pocket.

Valdez waved it off. "No need for that. I'll take him right now." He pulled out the shiny handcuffs from his belt.

"What?!" Leafblad shouted.

"I'm afraid you're coming with me tonight. Guess you already know that you have the right to an attorney. Let me go ahead and review the whole Miranda deal with you right now."

"This is absurd!" Pickney fumed loudly.

"That's a matter of opinion," Valdez replied.

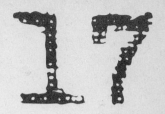

Justin hopped in his car and rushed over to the detention center in front of a parade of vans and cars—a reporter from the newspaper, then a cameraman and TV reporter, then another mob of the local press clogged the entrance. Men and women in business attire were coming along with a few cameramen in blue jeans and backward baseball caps burdened with broadcast video cameras. They looked like kids at the start of a gigantic Easter egg hunt storming in muttering about the brief statement Valdez had made to a radio station about the finding of the meeting. Justin overheard the barrage of questions thrown at Valdez.

"Is that a public school teacher in the back of your vehicle?" one reporter asked.

"What is his name?" another asked.

"Can you confirm reports that you are releasing the student who was framed for drug trafficking by a teacher at Summit High School?"

"Does this have anything to do with the computer theft at Summit that was reported last Sunday?"

Valdez smiled and said in a low voice, "All I need to tell you is that an innocent girl is being freed today. She has been totally exonerated. Other than that, I think you'll have to come to an arraignment and talk to a defense attorney or two because I'm not making any further comment."

"Are the D.A. and the police . . . are they trying to cover up . . . Is that why you don't want to comment further?"

"Nope. No cover-up." He scratched his head while rolling his eyes. "You'll get your story. I just don't want to talk to you right now. I'm tired, and I just want to do my job, so if you'll excuse me."

The reporters tried to provoke him, calling him a wimp and an obstruction of truth. But he had heard it all before and considered it a compliment. The press corp relaxed a bit as they tried to decide whether to stick around. Cars and newsvans filled the parking lot and lined the side of the road next to the detention center.

The word had spread like wildfire. Kandi would be released. Justin entered the building, along with Kandi's mom, Autumn, Melissa, Clipper, Shawn, and Jesse, their boss at the BurgeRama. After a few moments, other students and onlookers flooded the entrance. The doors remained open while people shifted and moved as if waiting for an important dignitary. The press went nuts over the drama that was unfolding. They tried to find a place for their cameras to record the event. Reporters screamed into cellular phones, urging their bosses and affiliates to give them the go-ahead for a live feed.

Autumn walked sneakily up to Justin, carrying a large brown grocery bag.

"Hey, Autumn. Pretty wild, huh?" Justin said.

"You got that right."

"Whatcha got there?" he asked casually.

Autumn pulled out a large arrangement of flowers, six long stem red roses garnished with tiny baby's breath blossoms and beautiful green leaves. Justin looked at her strangely. "Gee, Autumn, uh . . . thanks but . . . "

She hit him on the arm hard with her fist. "They're not for you, silly. I'm doing you a favor. She's had to put up with a lot from you."

Justin pointed his thumb at his chest innocently. "Me?"

"Yes, *you*. Darn right she has. I thought you might need a little help wooing her back. I really believe that guys have good intentions most of the time. Even you," she said smiling. "But you just don't have the skills or maybe the insight to follow through like you should. So I went out and got you these to give to Kandi when she gets out. She's going to think you're a really sensitive, romantic, and maybe worth her time. So when she comes out. Don't hug her. Don't pat her on the back and say 'great going kid.' Just look her in the eyes and hand her these. Say somethin' like, 'I'm so glad we're together. I've missed you, and I was a jerk for somehow getting you mixed up in all this.'"

"Wow, you're great. Thanks, Autumn," Justin said. "That was, well, the best thing a friend could do for me. But do I really have to tell her that I'm a jerk?"

"We love it when guys admit they're jerks. It's so romantic."

"Really?"

"Really."

Justin was very concerned. Kandi had been through a lot of humiliation and pain. Could she endure such a scene? The guard returned and opened the heavy steel door. A huge cheer greeted Kandi the moment she came into view.

She hugged her mom tightly, looking over her shoulder at all her friends assembled there to support her. Kandi's tired eyes lit up when she saw Justin. At that moment she knew the nightmare was over. They embraced, then Justin took Autumn's advise. He looked her in the eyes and said, "I missed you and I'm sorry for . . . uh . . . being a jerk and getting you mixed up in all this."

"No problem. But next time you go to the detention center. Deal?"

"Deal," Justin said as he looked around at the scene that surrounded them. He whispered in her ear, "Just one question. How'd you know about Felix's tape recording?"

"It was a shot in the dark. I saw Felix listening to his tape in the supply closet right before I got busted. He was crying, and I wasn't sure, but I thought I heard Leafblad's voice on the tape. He ran away from me. I've never seen him so scared, so I knew something was up."

Friday night at the BurgeRama, Autumn, Clipper, Justin, and Kandi teased each other as usual.

"You've got to admit, though," Clipper said in a business-like manner. "You know it *has* been a good night, Jesse. We've had such a huge night that I imagine that the BurgeRama is probably going to make a pretty penny off increased sales. Think we might get a raise?"

"Oh come on, Clipper. I know you're not really interested in money. You said last week you just do it for the fun of it," Jesse, their boss said, never looking up from his inspection sheet.

"And you thought I was serious!" Clipper replied.

"Pipe down you guys!" Justin said as he ran over to the television in the dining room. He stood on a chair and turned the volume up. A still shot of Leafblad on the monitor caught his eye. The other employees gathered around the set.

". . . and it is believed that the Summit High School robbery case has been officially closed as high school teacher Leafblad pled no contest to charges of robbery, willful destruction of public property, concealment of evidence, drug possession, commerce of stolen property, and blackmail. This plea has rocked the Summit community as Leafblad, who has taught for over twenty years, was the recipient of many teaching accolades, including Teacher of the Year. Apparently the teacher and an unnamed student burglarized the school and made the incident look like the actions of a rival Indianapolis high school. When a group of students discussed suspicious actions they had witnessed, he retaliated by planting drugs in one of the student's lockers."

The report continued with a sound bite from the head of press communications for the police department. "We received an anonymous tip that drugs and perhaps even a gun could be found in a student's locker at Summit High School on Tuesday. We took the tip seriously, so we conducted a search. However, we found no gun. After listening to the anonymous tip several

times with the help of voice imaging experts, we became convinced it was Leafblad who called. But let me repeat, there was
no gun ever in the school. We just believe it was his way of
forcing us to get the canine on the hunt."

The reporter appeared once more on the screen. "Kandi
Roper, age sixteen, was released and exonerated of all
charges." Kandi appeared on the screen being released in front
of the cheering overflow crowd with Justin handing her the
flowers. Autumn whispered to Justin while the others watched
in gleeful amazement. "See, I told you. The flowers did the
trick. You've got to admit, it was a stroke of genius. The flowers, I mean. She thinks you're great."

Justin smiled and whispered out of the corner of his mouth,
"The flowers? Nah, just my Brad Pitt looks and Robin Williams
sense of humor."

"Yeah . . . right," Autumn said sarcastically. "And I guess I'm
Whitney Houston."

Kandi broke in, "What are you two talking about?"

"Just talking, Kandi," Justin replied.

Kandi smiled and looked out of the door. "Hey, Clip, we've
got a customer."

Clipper looked over and saw Jenny knocking at the door.
His heart began to race. His palms broke out in sweat.

Jenny waved and smiled. She stood with one hand on her
hip and a finger curled around a belt loop on her jeans.

"Are you going to just wave, or are you gonna let her in,
Clipper?" Jesse said and laughed.

Clipper looked panicked. "I locked the door ten minutes
ago! Where are the keys?"

Justin patted him on the shoulder and waved at Jenny. "Buddy, I believe you left 'em in the door."

"You know, for a best friend, you can really be a jerk sometimes," Clipper said nervously.

"Yeah, that's what Autumn says about all us guys," Justin said half joking.

Autumn rolled her eyes. "Context, guys. There you go again, taking me out of context."

"Hi, everybody!" Jenny said as the door opened.

Everyone in unison waved and said, "Hi, Jenny," then pretended to work, keeping one eye on the situation.

Jenny looked up at Clipper and said, "I don't want anything to eat. I just had to let you know that I thought what you guys did this week was great." She turned to Clipper and pointed her finger into his boney rib cage. "I heard you were in that meeting with Leafblad and Lester. I don't think I could have done that. It must have taken a lot of courage."

"Yep, he was right in there with the rest of us," Justin said.

Clipper couldn't believe he had her attention. But she gave it to him undividedly. He could smell her subtle perfume, and it made him even more nervous. He was speechless, breathless, helpless, and hopeless.

"I came to ask you something, and I hope you don't think it's weird."

"What's that?"

Jenny put her hands in her pockets. "I don't know you that well, and I'm a sophomore."

"Right," Clipper confirmed, wondering where in the world this was heading.

"And you're a junior."

"Right," Clipper said.

Jesse turned down the Elvis Costello piped through the ceiling speakers so everyone could overhear some of the conversation.

"Somebody told me that you really want to go out with me."

Kandi, Autumn, and Justin tried to hide the fact that they were totally freaking out over this new development.

Clipper stood there stunned. "Well, as a matter of fact, I almost called you the other night to talk to you about that."

"But you couldn't find our number could you?"

He shook his head.

"It's unlisted. That's why."

"Oh," Clipper said, still only using one syllable words in his love struck stupor.

"But I think that would be fun," Jenny said.

"What?" Clipper asked. He couldn't believe this conversation.

"Going out."

"Who?" Clipper said obliviously.

"Us," Jenny replied.

"Us?"

"Yes. You don't want to?"

"Of course. Yes! I do! When? Where?" Clipper asked.

Jenny laughed. "Let's try this again. Why don't you start?"

"OK. Jenny, would you want to go out with me . . . uh . . . tomorrow night?"

"I'd love to! Call me." Jenny handed him her phone number on an index card. "Don't lose this or you're in trouble," she said with sassy smile. She turned around and walked out.

Clipper stood still as a statue, stunned silly.

The three friends cheered as he collapsed onto the floor. "He did it!" Justin yelled at the top of his lungs, loud enough to make Jenny turn around outside and peer through the window. What a climax to an unforgettable week.

Together they had everything they needed to survive. They had each other. They had God. That was enough.

Thanks for visiting Summit High. I'd love to hear from you if you ever want to ask a question, swap stories, need prayer, or even vent about life in general. My E-mail address is mtullos@bssb.com

See ya!
Matt Tullos